Nochebuena

A HOLIDAY NOVELLA

STEPHANIE SHEA

Edited by Crystal Wren.

Content Warning*: This book references the death of a parent, which is mentioned only as backstory and without detail.*

Acknowledgments

Say, my love, my best friend, I'll never be able to put it all into words, but I promise to never stop trying. *Siempre y para siempre.*

Lauren, thank you for always getting it, and for always being ready to throw on your proofreader cap for me. Let's resolve to keep those to-do list a little more manageable next year.

Laura, thank you for the priceless beta commentary that keep me laughing and spur me on. Ours is still one of my favorite examples of serendipitous friendships.

S-Jay, thank you for your never ending kindness and support. Let's get those words out of the notebooks and into the world!

Crystal, thank you for taking the time to edit another of my silly little kissing books.

And to my readers: This journey grows more surreal every day. Thank you for joining me on the ride.

Chapter 1

THE LEGAL DISSOLUTION OF A MARRIAGE

The percussive tap of stilettos against hardwood echoed Cami's tread back to her office, a stark contrast to the muted pat of men's Oxfords trailing her path. The door clicked shut behind her, but the wall of windows baring her corner of Dimaano Law to anyone who so much as ventured by left her skin taut with agitation.

Now that she thought about it, open door—or wall, as it may be—policies were bullshit. Never mind the fact that her boss, Pedro, had offered to have her office remodeled and outfitted with concealed blinds the day she'd made partner. Wallowing in a grandiose fishbowl after the most upsetting lunch of her adult life was apparently her destiny, as an imminent separation was to be her parents'.

"*Thirty years.*" She plopped into the high-back task chair behind her desk, sliding one thigh over the other. "Thirty fucking years and they're just going to sign it away."

"Honey." Justin cocked his head to one side and slipped both hands into the pockets of his blue-gray pants. The glimmer in his eyes would be twice as infuriating if they hadn't been friends long enough for Cami to know he really couldn't help it. Not his kind smile, or stupidly handsome Charles Michael Davis looks, or the way every last one of his designer suits made him look like a walking Forbes cover. If they weren't both very married and very gay, this outlandish blend of dapper sincerity might've been a problem.

He opened his jacket, smoothing a hand over his red silk tie as he settled into one of two accent chairs on the opposite side of her desk. "These things happen. You know this." His eyes swept her office, past the open laptop on her desk toward the bookshelf-storage combo unit housing both her client files and spare outfits. One *literal* run-in with an intern's coffee was all it took. Lesson learned. "Cam, you handle these cases every day."

"This isn't a case, Justin. These are my parents." She dropped her head back, eyes squeezed shut as she debated lamenting out loud the gravity of *her parents* getting divorced. It wasn't like Justin didn't know. Martín and Lupe Morales were the reason Cami was still a self-proclaimed romantic even after years of separation, asset division, child custody, and visitation cases, never mind watching people who once swore for better or worse try to out swing each other in a litigious cage match.

Her parents were the reason she still believed the last few months of spotty communication and flickering passion was merely a phase for her and Sutton. A blip they'd look back on thirty years later when a couple of twenty-somethings brimming with new love asked them the secret to it all.

Fuck if she knew.

"I'm guessing this is a bad time to mention that your mom asked me to handle their case," said Justin.

Cami's eyes sprang open as she lurched upright. "I'm sorry, what?"

"She called after you left the bakery, and you know I can't say no to your mom, or her buñuelos."

"Justin!"

"It's an amicable separation. They still love each other. They're just not"—he bobbed his head from one side to the next—"*in love* anymore."

"Not in love anymore. *Hazme el favor.*" She scoffed, pushing out of her chair. "You say it like it's a switch they flipped off this morning before they left for work."

"That would be a gross oversimplification."

"Exactly," she snapped, brows dipping as her brain processed Justin's revelation from an entirely new, though equally annoying angle. "And if it's so damn amicable, why didn't she ask *me* to handle the paperwork?"

"Neither of us need me to answer that, because you know better," Justin deadpanned. He stood, sighing as he closed the gap to rest a hand on her shoulder. "Look, I'm not going to give you some spiel about how watching your parents get divorced as an adult comes with a whole different slew of problems than it happening when you're a kid. This is your world. You've given the advice about setting healthy boundaries and acknowledging your feelings, which you clearly have a head start on," he said with a chuckle.

Her eyes flicked skyward in a playful roll. "I'm nothing if not proactive."

"Take it as a good sign that they're not fighting over who gets the house, or where Christmas is going to be."

"Oh my God. Where *is* Christmas going to be?" Cami's eyes widened. Nochebuena only happened once a year, and her family wasn't the house-hopping type. Every Christmas, her tíos, countless primos, her sister, nieces and nephew, and whoever else they'd collected along the way would gather under her parents' roof in the Mission. It was loud and hysterical, and there would be at least one argument, but it was *Nochebuena*. It was the scent of cinnamon, guava, and piloncillo syrup, and Luis Miguel streaming from a decades-old stereo.

It was also the closest to going home for the holidays that she got, being someone who saw her parents practically biweekly.

"Who announces their divorce two weeks before Christmas?" she grumbled. "I bet it was Papi's idea. He was never great with logistics."

Justin held up his thumb and index finger, squinting at the gap left between them. "I'm going to go out on a limb and say Luci's taking the news a smidge better than you are."

"Doesn't she always?" Cami's tone was only slightly begrudging. She admired her sister's resilience, marveled at her ability to juggle three kids, a husband who sometimes needed her more than they did, and manage the bakery full-time while never being phased by any of it. Lucia Morales was a certified superhero. Cami still resented that their parents had clearly told her first. The gasp she tried to pass off as surprise when Mami dropped the news couldn't trick a preschooler.

Cami released a heavy breath, the riot of emotions in her head gradually losing steam. "I know I'm being dramatic."

"Self-awareness *is* one of your better qualities." The corners of Justin's mouth quirked in a grin.

"I physically hate you."

"You love me," he countered, undeterred.

"I do." She heaved a sigh. "And I know we do this every day. I just didn't think it would ever be them, you know? It's because of them that what we do doesn't faze me. Papi still makes her cafécitos three times a day, and she sets timers on her phone to remind him to take his pills. They look at each other the same way they did when I was fifteen, Jus, even at lunch earlier. This is—" She stepped back, shaking her head as she sat on the edge of her desk. "I don't get it. And if this can happen to *them*, if they can break after three decades of love and commitment, do the rest of us even stand a chance?"

Justin winced, his eyes narrowing with concern. "Have you talked to her? Sutton."

"I've been trying to find the right time to bring it up, but —" Cami cut herself off, collecting her thoughts. She didn't want to reiterate how she and Sutton had been so out of sync, they were little more than passing trains these days. Stuck in a routine of small talk during breakfast prep, the odd midday text trail left forgotten the moment one of them had to rush into a meeting, followed by stunted recaps of their day they were often too exhausted to even enthusiastically complain about. She couldn't help feeling like somehow it should be easier for her—a twenty-eight-year-old family law attorney—talking to her wife about a marital slump. But as foreboding as the idea of prolonging things as they were seemed, broaching the topic only to have Sutton affirm that things weren't working, that she wanted time or space or a fucking divorce, was ten times more paralyzing.

"But what?" Justin dipped his chin in search of her gaze.

"Nothing. We've been busy. She just got promoted to director, and you know how intense my caseload has been since Pedro started taking less clients."

"About as intense as mine, except Brady demands that I leave work at the office. You and Sutton should try it."

"Cute." Cami schooled her face into a saccharine smile. He was right, but giving him shit was her love language.

"You don't get to give me advice when you're basically a newlywed."

"We've been married for nearly a year."

"Weak rebuttal, Nichols. Definitely shouldn't bring that energy to your next hearing."

His hand darted up, index finger pointing comically at her as he opened his mouth to argue, but the muted beep of his watch drew him up short, demanding his attention instead. His expression sobered as his eyes met hers. "That's the reminder for my three o'clock. I need to go over the case file before she gets here."

"Go." Cami bobbed her head toward the door. "I was getting sick of your face anyway."

Justin mimicked a hair flip, the action made more ridiculous by his closely cropped hair and basso tenor. "Oh, the perils of being beautiful."

A laugh bloomed in Cami's chest as she watched him leave. Not for the first time, she was grateful her best friend was only two doors down at work and never more than a phone call away. The last few months had been a whirlwind of baffling emotions and feeling worlds away from the person she shared a bed with every night. The person she still loved, wanted, more than anything or anyone. News of her parents' divorce was threatening to suck her deeper into the vortex of disillusion she'd been trying to outrun. She could always count on Justin to pull her out, but even he couldn't fix this one.

Besides, work was one thing, but she wasn't naïve enough to think her and Sutton being busy was all there was to the distance between them. It was more than that. She just didn't know what it was.

And how the hell was she supposed to fix something that she couldn't even name?

Chapter 2

DINNER FOR ONE

The clatter of keys against marble and a mumbled swear welcomed Cami home. She breathed a quiet laugh, blindly shutting the door behind her as she craned her neck to see beyond the short entryway to where Sutton stood by the kitchen island, rummaging through her favorite tote bag. Sutton Davies was as proper and polished as it got, but swearing was still her favorite form of self-expression.

Cami lowered her briefcase to the end table as she passed, her sigh riddled with exhaustion as much as relief. Even with the melee of fears and concerns that had trailed her home, seeing her wife after long days, having her close, never failed to ease the weight on Cami's shoulders. "You wouldn't believe the day I've had."

Sutton's hands stilled, her dark coffee eyes meeting Cami's only for a second before she resumed her search. "Work?"

"Among other things." Cami ventured closer, her gaze trailing a path from the wavy, raven locks swept into an artfully messy bun, the form-fitting dress Sutton had worn to the office this morning now replaced by a loose halter top, high-waisted pants, and Chelsea boots. But it was the golden necklace contrasting her sepia-toned skin that held Cami's stare, the same one Sutton had scarcely taken off since Cami had given it to her five years ago. If she closed her eyes, wished for it hard enough, maybe some unspoken force would whisk them back.

Pier 7 at sunset. Lanterns flickering on along the boardwalk as the day faded—the sky a misty kaleidoscope of burnt orange, pink hues, and soft blues. Sutton's laugh when the wind picked up and a strand of her hair caught on the latch of the necklace as Cami put it on. That laugh. Cami's favorite laugh. Infectious. Carefree. Heart-stopping.

She reached out, her fingers closing around the S-shaped pendant as nostalgia swelled in her chest.

Sutton's gaze followed the motion, but lines creased her forehead and she frowned. "Have you seen my AirPods?"

Cami's lips thinned as she slinked back, dropping her hand. "No. Did you check the thing?"

"The thing?" Sutton scratched her temple.

"The one on the nightstand, where you always—"

"Oh, yeah. They're not there." She zipped her bag shut with a shake of her head, pausing to lean closer—as close as she could get with the corner of the counter between them—and pressed a practiced kiss to Cami's cheek. "I have to run. Have dinner without me?"

"Wait." Cami grabbed her hand only for Sutton to face her with an exasperated pout.

"Babe, I'm late."

"So late you can't even pause to tell me where you're going when you just spent five minutes looking for your earphones?"

"Cam." Sutton tilted her head, the look in her eyes telegraphing something along the lines of *that's not fair*.

It would've worked, except Cami wasn't really interested in fair at the moment. "Are you even going to ask *why* my day sucked? I mean, beyond the default work answer."

"Yes, of course. Just—" Sutton's eyes drifted closed, and she drew in a steady breath before meeting Cami's gaze again. "Can we please talk about it when I'm back?"

"Back from?"

"My doctor's appointment. It's on the calendar."

Cami took a step closer, physically depriving herself of the space to consider the sharp decline in communication between them, so sharp they'd—or at least Sutton—had begun indiscriminately relying on words like *it's on the calendar*. Never mind the fact that this was her second "doctor's appointment" in as many weeks. Cami could almost envision the reply that would meet her concern, but it didn't stop the question from rolling off her tongue. "Is everything okay? I can come with you."

"No." Sutton shook her head, too fast. "Everything's fine, I promise. It's just a follow up." Her tongue swiped across her lips as her eyes flitted to Cami's mouth then met her stare. She leaned in, lips pillowing against Cami's so softly, the tenderness in that single, fleeting touch so rare these days, Cami's stomach ached with longing.

Sutton had always been able to placate her with a kiss. Once upon a time, it had even been their favorite way of calling timeout, a prelude to a level of intimacy that had been so intrinsic to how things used to be, she was terrified they'd never get it back. A montage of frenzied turned gentle kisses, knowing hands and breathless pleas flipped through her mind, filling her with a yearning so deep, the door had shut behind Sutton before Cami even realized...

The soft notes of musk and lavender lingering in the air wasn't Sutton's perfume.

Chapter 3

IMPOSTER

Fading rays of daylight streamed in from the open pair of bay windows, casting a glow over sage green walls. Sutton shifted on the loveseat, pinching the nylon fabric between her fingers. Six weeks. Six weeks and every time she set foot in this room with its built-for-comfort furniture and landscape artwork, she still couldn't shake the feeling that she wasn't supposed to be here. She'd read somewhere that fish tanks classified as positive distractions, a way to give the brain a break of sorts, but she still couldn't bring herself to look that one translucent, spotted fish in the eye. Marine life was terrifying, and humans had zero business fucking around in the ocean.

"Have you told Camila you've been seeing me?"

She resisted the urge to wince as her eyes met those of the woman seated in the armchair opposite her, pen hovering above the notepad on her lap. "Do you have to say it like that?"

"Like what?" asked Dr. Copeland, voice ever-even.

"Like it's something illicit, or..." This time, Sutton did wince. "Wrong."

"Is that how you think of therapy? As something illicit. Wrong."

"No. I just meant..." She trailed off, reassessing her words at the pair of studying eyes trained her way, discerning ears set to pick apart her every word for an underlying meaning. Even after scouring the internet for a highly regarded Black, queer therapist, someone she could relate to, who might relate to her, the idea of being shrinked made her stomach quiver with restless apprehension. So she didn't enjoy having someone root around her head, but she certainly didn't think there was anything wrong with it. "No," she repeated. "I don't think therapy is wrong."

"But you haven't told your wife," said Dr. Copeland, matter of fact.

"I don't want her to worry."

"She might be worried anyway. You mentioned that you two haven't been connecting the way you used to."

"I did."

Dr. Copeland tilted her head, her brows furrowed. "Why do you think that is?"

Maybe it was in Sutton's head, but her voice had softened on that question, her expression verging on welcoming. The whole thing made Sutton's scalp prickle. "I don't know."

"Do you have a theory?"

"A theory?" Sutton balked. "You mean, have I devised a dissertation topic for why I'm suddenly having trouble talking to the person I've shared everything with for the last five years? No. I don't have a theory, which is why I came to you."

Dr. Copeland scribbled a note, though her expression remained entirely neutral. "You seem agitated."

"I'm fine," Sutton groused.

"Do you blame yourself?"

"For feeling agitated?" Her brows shot up. "No. I blame this process, and maybe you, a little bit."

A chuckle drifted across the room, the doctor's full lips curved in a smile that faded almost as quickly as it had emerged. "We'll loop back to that one. My question was, do you blame yourself for the lost connection between you and Cami?"

Sutton bit the inside of her lip, one hand reaching up to twist the pendant on her necklace between her fingers. She'd gotten halfway to Dr. Copeland's office before it even occurred to her that it had been weeks since Cami last touched it, the look in her eyes so caring, nostalgic, despite the terrible day she'd had, and Sutton had been too distracted to notice. For what? Her fucking earphones and an appointment she'd been fifteen minutes early for anyway?

"We stopped having dinner together," she said. It wasn't the question Dr. Copeland had asked, but the words slipped out. "We stopped having dinner together because I started working longer days to get promoted. Then when I did, when I finally got the job I'd spent months chasing, I doubled down, because then I had to prove that I deserved it. I had to prove that it wasn't some desperate leap by the company to diversify their leadership team of geriatric white men, and *one* Asian woman they only hired last year." She scoffed, shaking her head. "I work hard. I'm good at my job. Some days, I'm fucking brilliant, but I still catch myself wondering if I deserved it, or if I was just some diversity pick."

"But you said it yourself, you're good at your job. Brilliant even," said Dr. Copeland. "Why wouldn't you deserve to be promoted?"

Sutton's shoulders slumped. She clenched her jaw, reducing her ire to a mumbled, "I don't know."

The woman hummed, scrabbling another line with her pen. "What did your father say when you told him?"

Sutton pursed her lips, eyes wandering to the fish tank. Positive distraction, she reminded herself. Expectedly, weird-looking fish didn't stop her father's words from clamoring in. "He said—" She swallowed, her throat taut with words she hadn't even uttered yet. "He said if I'd gone to Johns Hopkins, like he told me to, I'd be an attending by now."

Copeland narrowed her eyes. "How did you feel about that?"

"I kind of expected it." Sutton shrugged. "He's always been like that."

"He's always undervalued your accomplishments?"

"He's always been selective about which accomplishments deserve to be valued."

Another scribble. "You said you had to prove that you deserved the job. To whom? Your colleagues? Your father? Yourself or Cami, maybe."

"Cami believed I'd land that promotion before I did." She was the one who'd held Sutton's face in her hands, whisper-ranting, in Spanglish no less, how they'd be *pinche tontos* to pick anyone else. She was the one who'd kissed Sutton's anxiety into submission, at least until it wrangled free again.

"But you're suggesting the extra work has been difficult on your marriage," said Dr. Copeland. "Do you think that makes the problems you and Cami are having your fault?"

"We're not having problems. We just—"

"Haven't been connecting the way you used to. Right." A closed-lip smile graced the woman's faintly wrinkled face.

"I'd like you to try something before our next session. Set some time apart with Cami, schedule it if you have to, and do something you used to do together. It doesn't have to be elaborate or expensive, but it does have to be just the two of you. Then next week, let me know how it went."

"O-kay…" Sutton trailed off, hoping for more.

"Don't overthink it. There's no right or wrong outcome. It's just an exercise."

Just an exercise. Sutton turned over the words in her mind, but the implied simplicity wouldn't stick. There *was* a right outcome, one that had her senses dulling to the four walls of the room and nylon fabric beneath her fingers, awakening memories of weekend dates spent in museums after dark. Riding the Skunk Train through the redwoods, picnic basket and wine at the ready. Mornings when Cami would slip into Sutton's shower, setting her body aflame with a mere stroke of her fingers and starting something they couldn't finish in the thirty minutes before work, leaving Sutton all keyed up all day long. On the nights that followed, they wouldn't even make it to their bed. Not with Cami's mouth on hers the second she made it through the door, all excited laughter and bitten-off whimpers.

Moments like these, Sutton missed the sex almost as much as she missed the intimacy of after, when they'd lie wrapped up in each other, tracing indecipherable shapes on hips and thighs, kissing like time would stand still for as long as they stayed lost in each other's eyes. She missed the taste of *I love you* on Cami's lips, even if they still said it every day.

"Looks like you landed on something," Dr. Copeland hedged.

"No." Sutton shook her head, wincing as she sat up straighter. "Maybe. I don't know."

"That's fine. We'll talk about it next week." Copeland nodded, her expression softening as she glanced at her notepad again. "I'd like to loop back to your relationship with your father for a minute. To what you said about him being selective about which accomplishments deserve to be valued. Would you say it's been that way since you were very young?"

"Yeah, but he was just as hard on my brothers."

"Your brothers. Michael and..." Another note-check. "Matthew. Also doctors, as was your mother, before she passed. I imagined that set a high bar."

"I got used to the comparisons." Sutton channeled every ounce of rationale she possessed into the words, into her feelings about her father. Losing her mom at four years old had left her saddled with a lifetime of emotions she still didn't know how to process, let alone explain. "I guess my dad figured that was the easiest way of making his point."

"And what point was that?"

"He has these ideas of who I'm supposed to be. A surgeon or a tech mogul, or whatever. Anything less involved is a"—she primed her fingers to make air quotes and resisted the urge to scoff at the complete absurdity of it —"waste of my brain. Whatever the fuck that means."

Lines creased the space between Dr. Copeland's brows. Sutton anticipated another swift pass of pen over paper. Instead, the woman tilted her head, looking at Sutton more intently as she cupped one hand over the back of the other. "Sutton..." She hesitated, almost as if she hadn't fully committed to uttering the words dancing on her tongue. And then, with the same measured care with which she spoke every word, she asked, "Are you familiar with the term imposter syndrome?"

Chapter 4

OPERATION ROMPOPE

Clammy palms fumbled across Sutton's face, patting and squishing in anarchy as adorable green eyes beamed up at her. Between the episodic spit bubbles and blissful babbling, it was safe to assume that Pablo was still just as in love with her as he'd been last week, but a little reassurance always did wonders for her mood, even if he somehow managed to get heavier by the second.

She adjusted him on her hip, scrutinizing the counter where a blob of dough had his mom occupied. A fragrant medley of cinnamon, guava, and anise lingered in the air, though the bakery had been closed for well over an hour. It wasn't December at Dolce until the scent of freshly baked buñuelos coursed her veins with every breath. Still...

"Aren't you usually done with prep by now?" she asked.

Luci peered up through long, dark lashes, the same ones that made Sutton's belly swoop every time Cami's eyes fluttered open first thing in the morning. "We *are* usually done with prep by now, but apparently when you're a mom of three, running a—"

Sutton's free hand darted to Pablo's ear as she held him closer to her chest.

"—*fucking* bakery during the holidays, some things slip through the cracks. Things like how I promised Sofi's school four dozen chocolate chip cookies for their fundraiser tomorrow. Considering I've been here since three a.m. and I'm running on, like, five hours of sleep, I'm very angry with the person I was when I committed to this."

Sutton bit down on a laugh. "I say this with the security of holding your last-born child as a human shield, but you could've just picked up some cookies at Trader Joe's. It's not like the school would know the difference."

"Not like the school would know the—" Luci's hands stilled as she narrowed her eyes at Sutton. "Bring my baby over here."

"He's good. Aren't you, Pablito?" She nuzzled her nose to his cheek, melting a little when he squealed and tried to squirm out of her grip. "See? I think he even agrees with me."

"Whatever. The only reason I'm not pelting you with my top tier, homemade cookie dough is because Chema's up to his knees in Styrofoam balls thanks to Regi's solar system project, and you saved my ass by getting Pablo from daycare."

"Really? That's the only reason? Not our decade-old friendship?"

"No, because you've been a little shit for every last year of it."

"Jesus, Luce." Sutton covered Pablo's ears again. If there was anything she and Luci had in common, it was their knack for swearing, but at this rate, Pablo would be cursing before his second birthday.

"Oh, he's heard worse. It's his grandparents you have to

worry about. They think he won't latch onto the Spanish ones but any odds his first word is *pende—*"

"*Don't* finish that," Sutton rushed out through a laugh. Even so, it took a moment for Luci's words to truly set in, for it to occur how much was about to change for their family, and how Sutton and Cami had barely talked about any of it. "Are they really getting divorced?"

"Seems like it," said Luci, her tone verging on somber. "I don't love it. I'm not even a hundred percent sure what it means for them, or for us. But it's not like there's anything we can do about it, no matter how much Cami kicks and screams."

Sutton pursed her lips. Two nights ago, when she'd gotten home from therapy—her mind a mess of thoughts about her father, words like imposter syndrome, Dr. Copeland's suggestion that she carve out time to do something for her and Cami—Cami had been so subdued, there hadn't been much kicking and screaming at all. Not that Sutton didn't know she was hurting. She idolized her parents' marriage, held them as the pinnacle of what true, lasting love should look like. But when Sutton had probed, asking whether something had happened or if Lupe and Martín had said why they were getting divorced, Cami had curled farther into her side of the bed, mumbling words that vaguely resembled, *I don't know. I don't know anything anymore.*

Pablo wriggled, jerking Sutton back to the present. She pressed a hand to his little round belly, rocking from side to side as she mumbled endearments against his cheek. When her gaze drifted back to the kitchen, inquisitive brown eyes awaited hers.

"You want to tell me where you were just now? You completely checked out."

"It's nothing," said Sutton.

Luci arched a brow, bracing both palms on the counter. "Let's try that again."

"I don't—" Sutton grimaced, forever battling her brain's impulse to internalize. They hadn't exactly made it to that module of therapy yet, but there was something about speaking her feelings out loud that made her want to disappear, if only so she wouldn't have to process the look on peoples' faces in the aftermath. But this was Luci. Luci who she'd been friends with since their junior year in college, who never sugarcoated, or pitied, and had certainly never treated her like she was made of glass. "I'm worried she's not talking to me. I'm even more worried it's my fault, or that I've run out of chances to be hung up on work or so *fu*—" She bit down on the word, eyes darting to Pablo, and okay, maybe it *was* harder than it seemed. Not swearing. "I shut down. I get overwhelmed and I internalize, and I shut down. I know that. But I'm trying to fix it. I spend an hour a week, on my ass, literally learning how to deal with things any person my age already knows how to talk about, and that's fine. I hate it, but I'll do the work. I can do the work, Luce, but I can't..." Her eyes fell shut as she shook her head, catching her breath. "I *can't* lose *her*."

"You won't." Concern glimmered in Luci's stare, but she spoke with conviction.

"Have you—" Sutton winced, her stomach churning with mounting desperation. "You haven't told her, right? About picking me up that day."

"No. It's not really my thing to tell, S." Luci sighed, grabbing a towel to rub at the remnants of dough clinging to her fingers as she rounded the counter between the bakery's lobby and kitchen, then closed the distance between them. "Look, I'll be the first to admit that you two have been a little... *off*, lately. I've been trying to stay out of it because trouble in paradise between my sister and best friend is the kind of minefield literally no one should have to maneuver. But I know you, and I know her, and neither of you are even close to being done. The second you get your heads out of your asses and actually talk to each other, you'll be back to sneaking off to fucking coat closets and disappearing for whole weekends without a word to anyone."

Sutton's brows twitched with uncertainty as her gaze drifted toward Dolce's main entrance, beyond the glass panes to her parked SUV. A weekend getaway to Napa or Tahoe. Maybe that would've been a better idea. Or would it have been presumptuous to even assume Cami would want to drop everything and go, given how rickety things had been between them lately? It wasn't like Cami hadn't been swamped at the firm too. She just happened to be better at compartmentalizing than Sutton had ever been.

"I'm going to talk to her." Sutton's nod was more for her own benefit than Luci's. "I just... Dr. Copeland suggested something, and I think it might help us reconnect a bit. Get rid of some of the tension so it's not so stilted and weird when we actually talk."

Luci's eyes narrowed to slits. "Get rid of the tension?"

"Not like that," Sutton drolled, feigning exasperation. It didn't stop her skin from flushing, hairs on her nape rising at the very thought.

Luci's gaze drifted to the main entrance. "Does it have anything to do with the tree strapped to the roof of your car?"

"It might." A smile tugged at Sutton's lips.

"Well, given how obsessed Cami's been with Christmas since we were kids, I'd say you're on the right track."

"I honestly don't know how we made it to the fifteenth without a tree in the house. We don't even have lights up."

Luci shrugged. "You've both been busy. It happens."

"I guess." Sutton bit the inside of her cheek, resisting the urge to mumble that it was mostly her. Self-flagellation might be a bad habit she'd yet to break, but Luci wouldn't have any of it. Instead, Sutton flinched beyond the reach of the tiny fingers clawing at the diamond stud in her ear and bounced Pedro on her hip. "I actually need your help. I know you've already been here all day and you're wrecked, but I'll owe you. Like, take-the-kids-for-a-full-weekend owe you."

Luci's brows inched up, the smile curling her lips downright villainous. "All three?"

"No. Just the two I like." Sutton scoffed. "Yes, Luce. All three, obviously."

"Deal."

Sutton's gaze flickered to the outstretched hand awaiting hers. "You're not even going to ask what I need?"

"You underestimate how much I need a weekend away from all of this." She waved her hand in a sweeping gesture toward the kitchen before settling on Pablo, wiggling her fingers against his side and spawning a new fit of squeals and squirming. "Including my very cute kids."

"You know you could just ask us to watch them sometimes. Cami insisted I couldn't turn the spare room into a mini gym, because 'what about when the kids sleep over?'"

"Yeah, but you two have enough going on as it is. Besides, how do you know I'm not storing all my kid-favors for a big cash out?"

Sutton bobbed her head from side to side, considering it. "Calculated with a dash of evil genius. Yeah, that tracks."

"I try." Luci chuckled, feigning nonchalance. "Really, though. What do you need?"

"Cami's at Justin's, which buys me a little time until she gets home to get everything ready, but I need Rompope. Like, Familia Morales secret recipe Rompope."

"Ohhh." A shit-eating grin crept onto Luci's face as she nodded slowly. "And you couldn't have just picked some up at Trader Joe's? It's not like Cami will know the difference."

"Listen." Sutton shifted Pablo to her other hip before holding up her free hand in contrition. "I fully acknowledge the irony and error of my earlier comment. I stand before you a changed woman, one who's still willing to look after this angel and his two older sisters any weekend of your choice."

Luci dropped her head back, a vibrant cackle flooding the bakery, warming Sutton from the outside in. "You underplayed your hand. I still don't forgive either of you for sneaking around for months before telling me you were dating, but you happen to be my favorite couple. I would've made it for free." She pressed a kiss to Pablo's cheek then bopped Sutton on the nose with a finger. "*But* I'll let you know which weekend I'll be collecting."

Sutton laughed, shaking her head. There were several reasons why Luci would always be one of her favorite people, but the heart of gold shrouded beneath layers and layers of snark and blasé topped the list. "Fine," Sutton agreed, holding up a finger, "but don't just show up with diaper bags at seven a.m. one day. I expect at least two weeks notice."

"Come on, S." Luci tsked, glancing over her shoulder as she started for the kitchen. "You're married to a lawyer. Don't you know you're supposed to talk terms *before* making a deal?"

Chapter 5

PONTE LAS PILAS

The recessed lights beaming from Justin and Brady's living room ceiling did nothing for the incessant pounding in Cami's head, neither would the can of beer in her hand. Still, the trio of throw pillows piled between her shoulders and neck were comfortable enough to make her question staying on this sofa all night. Scratch that. All weekend.

Justin plopped onto the adjacent sofa, his own can of beer in hand. "I still can't believe she lunged across the table. I swear you get all the exciting mediations."

Cami scoffed. That was one way of putting it. She smothered the urge to say she'd take every last one of Justin's less eventful arbitrations, because two women descending into a slap fight over who should get the original *Dumas* hanging in what used to be their living room wasn't the kind of excitement she craved right now. Or ever. Even with the needs of her client paramount, she'd been too preoccupied to intervene.

A tornado of her worst fears had been ripping through her for days, the same whirlwind of lavender perfume spinning her round and round, so dizzying she could barely think straight. Musky and sweet and—

"Have you ever cheated on Brady?" she blurted.

A gurgled, choking sound escaped Justin, forcing Cami to sit up and face him. Wide eyes glimmered back at her, one hand clamped over his mouth as the moment stretched, her anticipation and his perplexity meeting somewhere in the space between them. His brows inched closer together, and he slowly lowered his beer to the coaster on the coffee table before reaching for a paper napkin to dry his lips. "You're serious?"

"Obviously whatever you tell me stays between us," said Cami. "I won't even tell Sutton."

"Put aside the fact that I've known you way too long to believe there's anything you don't tell Sutton, there's nothing to tell. Brady and I were open when we started dating, but even then, I wasn't seeing anyone else."

"Do you think he ever was?"

Justin flinched, shaking his head. "Cami, what is this about? Did you meet someone?"

"What?" Outrage slipped into her tone. "No, of course not."

"So… this is about Sutton?" he asked carefully.

Cami's gaze dropped to the twist and flex of her fingers on her lap, her throat growing tighter by the second.

"Hey." Justin stood, crossing the space in two long strides to sit next to her, hands tucking braids away from her face as he dipped his head in search of her eyes. "You're spiraling. I mean this in the best possible way. Sutton is obsessed with you. Whatever's going on, I'm sure that's not it."

"That's what you're supposed to say. It's what I'd probably be telling you if this was reversed because I'd say anything—"

"Cam, I'd bet a year's salary on it."

She bit down on her bottom lip to stop the impending quiver. "She smelled like... lavender."

"What?" He blinked hard, glaring at her as if her words just didn't compute, or maybe because they'd barely slipped out.

Maybe she hadn't wanted to fuel them with the power of being spoken aloud, but keeping them bound and tangled up in her brain wouldn't make them any less real. All that had done was goad her imagination into spawning a caricature of the woman she loved with the phantom of another person—felt but never seen.

"She didn't smell like *her*. She smelled like someone else."

"There are a million explanations for that," said Justin.

The force of Cami's headshake was dizzying. "It's not just that. She has doctor's appointments she never explains, and other weird reasons for rushing off mid-conversation. Fucking doctor's appointments, Justin, as if that's the kind of thing I'm just supposed to ignore if it is true."

Justin held up a hand. "Okay, but—"

"Don't even get me started on the last time we had sex."

"Every couple goes through slumps," he argued.

"This is starting to feel like more than that."

"Have you tried talking to Luci? If anyone would know what's going on, it's her."

"You think she'd tell me?" Cami balked. "We may be sisters, but Sutton's always been her best friend."

"Luci would never sit by and let anyone hurt you. Not even Sutton." Justin shifted closer, their knees bumping as he took Cami's hands in his. "This isn't you. This isn't the Cami who ran into her sister's older, much more sophisticated, and totally intimidating friend, and won her over in a single night."

Cami's eyes drifted closed at the mere mention of it, every nerve in her body firing at the instant unraveling of memories. Five years, but she remembered it all in vivid detail. The shift from perplexity to kismet when Sutton glanced up from her phone, straightened raven hair tucked behind both ears, her sepia complexion radiant with reddish brown undertones, glowing even beneath the dull beam of the grimy ceiling lamp by the bar's entryway. The wrong bar. At least, not the kind of dive Sutton had expected to wander into, dressed like she was—light ivory colored coat skirting her knees, long slender legs garbed in skintight black jeans and designer boots.

Cami couldn't forget it if she tried. She couldn't forget the hours they'd lost strolling the sprightly streets of SoMA, or the way Sutton had gasped against her mouth, blunt nails scratching at hips when Cami had lost the battle to not kiss her.

The most surprising thing wasn't that Cami's memories hadn't faded in the least. It was the watery laugh that lurched from her throat, the hammering in her chest, tingling in her fingertips. "I'm a really good kisser," she joked.

Justin snapped his fingers, pointing at her. "Gonna take your word for it, but just in case you feel the need to tell me what else you're good at, please don't."

She fell back against the couch, her laugh morphing into a frustrated groan as she dragged both palms down her face. "I can't keep doing this. I genuinely think I'm going to lose my mind."

Fingers wrapped around her wrist, removing her hands and forcing her to meet Justin's eyes again. "Look, you know

I'll be here for whatever you need. No matter what. So trust me when I say I mean this with nothing but love, you need to go home, Cam. Talk to your wife. And don't call me, or Luce, or anyone until you can say with all honesty that you've tried."

Tension crept through her muscles like a slow-spreading paralytic, tightening her chest. It was simple advice. Good advice. She just—

"I know you're scared she'll say something that will shatter any hope of getting things back to the way they were." Justin's eyes gleamed with concern, his hands still resting on hers. "But you have to know. It's the only way through this."

He was right. She knew he was right, but still. "Would it have killed you to save this pep talk until after I was drunk?"

"Yes, because then you'd have an excuse to pretend you forgot it." He grinned, urging her on with a clap. "Come on. Ponte las pilas."

Cami sneered, rolling her eyes. "I'm so mad at my mom for teaching you that. A-plus on the pronunciation though," she added begrudgingly.

"I've been practicing." He reached for his phone, thumbs swiping across the screen for a quiet moment before his gaze drifted to her stocking-clad feet. "And please put your shoes on. Pretty sure going barefoot in a rideshare is still frowned upon."

"Jesus Christ, Justin. It was *one* time."

Chapter 6

BACK TO DECEMBER

Cami drew in a deep breath as she slotted her key into the lock and twisted. If their earlier text exchange was anything to go by, Sutton probably wasn't expecting her home yet. Not that she'd bothered to ask what time Cami would be leaving Justin's, never mind offering a sliver of insight about how she herself would be spending the night.

Now that Cami thought about it, she didn't know whether Sutton was home or an empty house awaited her. For all she knew Sutton was out with whomever had left their mark all over her two days ago. Except, it was like Justin had said, the person Cami loved—whose aloofness, poise, and amused head-tilt had bowled her over the second their eyes locked—would never, *could* never...

Fuck. She squeezed her eyes shut, forcing the thought down. Having an over-active imagination had done wonders for her in school, even still, but there were times she sincerely wished she could hit return to sender and have DHL show up on her doorstep to collect. Whether Sutton was here or not, she had one goal for tonight. She had to get the words out, even if she'd have to curl up in the armchair with their warmest throw blanket and her favorite book, and wait. With a steadying breath, she opened the door and went in, heeling off her shoes at the entrance.

The faint melody of music flowed through the entryway, soft lyrics riddled with reminiscence. A heady blend of pine, citrus, and spicier notes she couldn't quite name lingered in the air. Her brows dipped, her thoughts growing more jumbled with every cautious step. Something clattered, metal and plastic rattling against hardwood.

"*Shit.*"

Cami rounded into the living room to see Sutton grab a tumbling power wheel wrapped in fairy lights, then scramble to her feet.

"You're home." Everything from the breathless awe in her tone, raven curls escaping a messy top knot to frame her face, the sexy contrast of the tank top hugging her torso and loose flow of lounge pants ending in bare, manicured feet made Cami ache for the routine of moments before now. Moments when the certainty of what was would propel her straight into Sutton's arms until their lips touched. The softest brush of *hello*. "I tried to get it as close as possible to the one you wanted last year," said Sutton.

Cami blinked free of her haze. At least, she tried. "What?"

"The tree." Sutton waved toward it. "It's a Canaan Fir, which the guy said is some kind of hybrid?"

Cami followed her gaze to the towering tree, the teak wood base holding it in place a perfect contrast to the rich green foliage covering each branch. Partly opened boxes and cylinders of ornaments along with four—Cami frowned, no, six—potted nochebuenas in varying sizes took up half the living room floor.

Sutton inched closer, the movement drawing Cami's focus back to her, to the smile tugging at the corners of her mouth. "I was driving by the market, and I know you're the impulse buyer in this marriage, but this felt like a good reason for an exception. Plus, you were with Justin, and I know you had a hard week, so I didn't want to interrupt your plans."

"You didn't want to interrupt?" Cami uttered, still so far behind she couldn't begin to make sense of it.

"I mean, I figured I'd just wait until you got home. It's not like all this stuff's going anywhere."

"You were just going to wait?"

Sutton's brows dipped, almost as if it didn't occur to her why Cami would be so surprised. "I'll always wait for you. As long as you promise to always come home to me."

"Sutton..." Cami pressed a hand to her stomach, a futile effort to stave off the overwhelming mix of doubt and longing, never mind something she'd never felt looking at her wife. Mistrust? No matter how she spun it, she couldn't make sense of the suddenness of it all, and maybe the part of her she'd laid bare and exposed all these years was afraid to believe in it—to think it could be this easy, that she'd simply come home one night and everything would be okay. "I don't—what is this?"

"I know it's out of the blue." Sutton took another step. "I really was driving by the market, thinking about work and us and everything, and it hit me. It's the fifteenth. It's halfway through December and we didn't have a tree."

Cami let her eyes drift again. There hadn't been a single year since they'd moved in together when their apartment hadn't been robed in lights, tree ornamented and dazzling by the first day of the month. With everything else that had been happening, the absence of stockings on their mantle and citrusy menthol scent in the air had completely escaped her.

Sutton's final step left her so close the tips of their toes were touching. "I know we have a lot to talk about. I don't want to gloss over that, and if the abruptness of this feels completely absurd and gross and gas-lighty, I'll put it all away so we can talk right now." She wet her lips, shaking her head. "Or whenever you're ready. I just thought it might be nice to have one night to feel like us again."

Hope flared in Cami's belly, boundless and wild. Her eyes drifted shut, defenses she hadn't even realized she'd erected collapsing brick by brick as she leaned in, their noses brushing. She drew in a long breath, comforted by the hint of vanilla rose, subtle and sweet, not remotely like lavender. "A night to feel like us sounds perfect."

"Yeah?" Sutton's breath tickled her lips.

Cami curled a hand around her hip, holding her closer. "Yes."

Their eyes met, the seconds stretching as Sutton's gaze drifted lower then back, seeking confirmation before she softly pressed their mouths together. Cami let herself get lost in it—the silken skin beneath her palm, just above the waistband of Sutton's pants, tangy-sweet traces of wine on her tongue, the fingers threading through Cami's braids when she tilted her head to deepen the kiss. A hum reverberated between them, a precursor to the smile pressed against hers, and Sutton flattened her other hand against Cami's tensing abdomen, flicking a shirt button between her thumb and index finger before fisting her hand and reluctantly dropping it to her side.

"Um..." She licked her lips, breaths pillowing against Cami's cheek.

Cami's fingers tingled with the urge to find the back of

her neck, guide her lips back home, and never stop, not until she was naked and pliant beneath the weight of Sutton's body. But Sutton turned, Cami's hand in hers as she guided her toward the orderly mess of decorations.

"I got everything out, but obviously you're going to have to take the lead here."

A laugh bloomed in Cami's chest, and she squeezed Sutton's hand, if only to feel the sharp press of the diamond ring she still wore with her wedding band. "Four years of living together and you're still afraid to touch the tree without supervision?"

"I know my limits. Four years of you telling me exactly where to hang each ornament doesn't make up for decades of never even having a tree."

"I still can't believe your dad never put one up. I'd get it if he didn't believe in, well, any of this, but he still makes a big deal whenever you don't visit for the holidays."

"I don't think it's about the holiday. Probably just another warped expectation he needs us all to meet. You know how he gets." Sutton shook her head, smiling softly. "I don't want to spend my first Friday night with you in weeks talking about him. Tell me about you, about your day or something."

Cami debated probing further, but it had always been like dancing along a live wire, talking about Sutton's family. Overbearing dad, high-achieving siblings, a mom who died when Sutton was only four. Not that Cami's day was a promising alternative. Still, when she opened her mouth, her brain buzzing with possibilities to chase away the distance in Sutton's eyes, the words slipped out anyway. "I had a client lunge at her ex mid-mediation."

Sutton's hand stilled halfway to the power wheel

wrapped in lights, her eyes glinting with amazement and the faintest glimmer of mirth. "Really?"

"Yup. Took half the firm to separate them, because the only thing this case needs is an assault charge in the mix."

"Fuck. Is someone pressing charges?"

"Sure hope not." Cami scoffed. Maybe it was the intensifying shock on Sutton's face, or the complete absurdity of that moment in the conference room being just another day at the office lately, but a laugh ballooned in her chest, shifting the weight of everything else. Her parents' divorce, the fear of her and Sutton being next, lavender perfume and the looming ghost of someone else.

"God, I love that laugh," Sutton whispered.

Cami dropped both hands, though her grip tightened on the cord wrapped around her fingers. Her pulse picked up, steady but strong, and she tried to remind herself that as nice, as good as this felt, the fissures in their marriage couldn't all be sealed in a single night. Even with Sutton looking at her like that—eyes gleaming with love and something that vaguely resembled a contentment Cami missed with her entire being.

"I almost forgot." Sutton grinned, spinning on the balls of her bare feet, and heading for the kitchen. She swung one side of the fridge open and stuck her head in before emerging with a jug of creamy, yellow liquid in hand.

Cami edged closer, drawn in by the sweet blend of cinnamon, vanilla, and just a hint of rum. "You made Rompope?"

A soft chuckle resonated as Sutton lowered the jug to the counter and went in search of glasses. "Don't sound so worried. I didn't make it. Luce did."

"You asked Luci to make you Rompope?" Cami amended, no less incredulous.

"We may have to watch the kids for a weekend, but they're due for a visit anyway. Besides, I wanted to do this right. It's not tree-decorating night without Rompope."

She canted her head, squinting. "So you were planning this?"

"I'd use the word planning very lightly. That's why I didn't say anything when you told me you'd be at Justin's tonight, but I promise to give you more notice before the next one."

"The next what?"

"The next night or day we spend together." Sutton's gaze dipped to the glasses, though whether it was due to uncertainty or an effort not to spill the drink she was pouring, Cami couldn't be sure. Not until Sutton followed up with, "If you're up to it, I mean."

"If I'm up to it?" Cami's laugh echoed disbelief. Somewhere in the back of her mind, it occurred to her that she was merely repeating Sutton's words, but every answer left her more confused than the last, and she wanted to be in the moment. To enjoy it. She also needed to understand why. When Sutton offered her a near-full rocks glass, she resisted the urge to immediately indulge, lowering it back to the counter and moving to stand in front of Sutton instead.

She chewed her bottom lip, gaze trained on her fingers as they toyed with the strings on Sutton's lounge pants until the very second she needed to look her in the eyes. "I know you. I know you better than people who've known you all your life, which is how I know there's something else going on. Something you haven't told me. And I don't need you to, not until you're ready. Just promise me..." Her voice faded to a whisper. "Promise me this is some unpredicted but completely ordinary marital rite of passage, and that we'll be okay."

"Hey." Sutton framed her face with both hands, thumbs stroking her cheeks as their gazes held. "I know I've been preoccupied and"—she sighed, eyes flicking skyward—"stuck in my head all the time about work and whether they made the right decision with the promotion, and—"

"Don't even go there." Cami shook her head. Maybe she hadn't always liked what it took for Sutton to make director, the youngest director of a transnational research corporation. Maybe sometimes she even resented it, but there was no question that Sutton deserved it. "You *earned* that job."

"But I lost sight of this." Sutton's stare didn't waver. "It's funny. It took me years to get there, to get noticed, and I feel like I blinked and we were sleeping on different sides of the bed."

"We always slept on different sides of the bed," said Cami, amusement slipping into her tone.

"Maybe, but we always met in the middle. I guess..." Sutton shrugged. "I guess that's what this is. Me trying to meet in the middle. I missed this. Friday nights together, talking about everything and nothing at all, and kisses like *that*." She pointed to the spot they'd been standing in earlier, lips chasing each other, Cami's hands low on her hips, hers in Cami's hair. "Moments when you kiss me like you're just checking if you can still take my breath away."

Cami simpered, her heart hammering as the words washed over her. "Inquiry minds *would* like to know."

"The fact that I was seconds from trying to get you out of your clothes wasn't a giveaway?"

"I mean, I am still wearing them. A little reassurance seemed in order."

Sutton breathed a laugh as she inched closer, mouth ghosting a trail to Cami's ear, hands slipping around her waist. "I can tell you how many days it's been since you last came on my tongue. I could tell you you were wearing that black top with the viole sleeves that we got in Paris, the same one you haven't worn to work since because it's still missing two buttons. I could tell you how a week ago, in a meeting with the VP and half my team, I missed a whole segment remembering the exact way you said my name right before you came so hard I know our neighbors heard."

Cami's grip tightened on the edge of the counter, a gulp sliding down her throat.

"I could also tell you it's exactly what I thought about when I touched myself in the shower that night."

"Sutton..." Her breathing grew faster, her skin feverish at the mere recount, the images it stirred of Sutton's back pressed to the cold tiles of their shower, hand between her thighs, eyes closed and mouth open.

"I miss you," said Sutton, pulling back just enough for their eyes to lock. "I miss every inch of you. I just..."

"Tell me," Cami urged softly.

"I don't want it to ever feel like sex is the only good thing between us."

"That could never be true."

"Maybe." Sutton nodded, her fingers tracing up the back of Cami's neck, leaving goosebumps in their wake as she brought their foreheads together. "But I need you to know I mean every word. I'm in this, Cam. Not just for the easy parts, or because you can still wind me up with a single look. Because this *is* just some ordinary rite of passage, and you're so unbelievably stuck with me. Not for thirty more years. For a lifetime."

The words thirty years reverberated in Cami's head. They'd yet to have any in-depth conversation about her parents' divorce, but she couldn't help feeling like this was Sutton's way of saying they would set their own standard.

Even if the couple Cami had built her hopes and expectations on were calling it quits, that didn't mean she and Sutton wouldn't make it through this. Her eyes drifted closed, and she pulled Sutton closer. "A lifetime?"

"A fucking lifetime." Sutton shrugged. "Or at least until I'm eighty and pedantic, and you've absolutely had enough of my bullshit."

"See you're thirty-three and already way too pedantic so we're on thin ice as it is."

Sutton shook her head, lips brushing Cami's, stoking the flame in her belly. "On second thought just kiss me and forget I said anything."

She captured Cami's bottom lip between hers, but it was Cami who eliminated the last sliver of space between them, pressing Sutton against the counter at her back and tilting her head to deepen the kiss. It wasn't the talk Cami intended —not really—but tonight, it was enough. Soft music streaming from the surround sound, the air laden with pine and citrus, cinnamon and vanilla, the warmth of having her wife in her arms, and the calm of a Friday night ahead. For the first time all month, it felt like Cami's favorite time of year, one of the thousand reasons she'd always go back to December.

Sutton's lips curled against hers, eyes twinkling as she mumbled, "You think it's working?"

Cami hummed, pulling her back in by the collar of her shirt. "I don't know. I think you should try a little harder."

A laugh floated between them, infectious and airy, sending a shiver straight to Cami's toes. Sutton nodded, the tips of their noses touching. "For you... *always*."

Chapter 7

XO, CAM

Sutton curled closer to the warmth engulfing her, into the arm wrapped around her waist. A puff of air caressed her neck, and she hummed, goosebumps pebbling her skin as she drifted out of sleep. "Hi." It came out sleep-addled and scratchy, but Cami had always loved that about her voice first thing in the morning.

Cami's arms tightened, pulling her closer. "How do you always smell this good?"

"One of the many benefits of nighttime showers?" said Sutton, glib. She knew the question didn't demand an answer so much as it was the affectionate mumblings of her wife on a cozy December morning. "It's also better for your skin and sleep and—"

"Ha-ha. You're hilarious." One hand cradled her face as Cami hovered above her, and their lips brushed, the touch so faint, so evanescing, Sutton was powerless to do anything but roll onto her back and chase it.

But Cami faded into a watercolor of dark braids, warm brown skin, and gleaming eyes, pixelating and floating off into an invisible void.

Sutton's eyes fluttered open to the blank plane of her ceiling, and she turned to find the other side of the bed empty, contrary to the dream she'd been having seconds ago. Rumpled sheets averred Cami's absence, though the memory of her falling asleep in Sutton's arms was so fresh Sutton could still smell the rosy scent of her hair—an unapologetic little spoon though she had at least three inches on Sutton without heels.

"Cam?" She glanced toward the open closet, then the en suite.

When only silence answered, she swung her legs over the edge of the bed, and her gaze snagged on the purple note on the nightstand. Three months. It'd been three months since she'd woken to one of these. An affirmation, an *I love you*, a request that she wear a particular pair of underwear to work. Lace instead of cotton.

She reached for the paper, heart racing as she flipped it over to scan the words.

Charlie called out sick and Luci needed help opening.
I didn't want to wake you.
Be home as soon as I can.
XO, Cam.

Sutton blew out a breath, falling back onto her pillows. So much for her plans for breakfast in bed. Not that she expected things to be that simple because they'd had a good night. She closed her eyes as Cami's laugh echoed in her head, gleeful, almost childlike, when Sutton broke rank to wrap *her* in fairy lights instead of following her directives about where to put them on the tree. Never mind the yelp she made as she tumbled onto the rug, bringing Sutton down with her, and leaving the box of stockings trapped beneath their weight—a casualty to their antics.

After hours of lights, ornaments, and hysterical laughter between *no, babe, it's still not straight* and *fine, I'll do it*, they'd been too full on Rompope and midnight pizza to do anything but fall asleep in each other's arms. As her breathing slowed and she began to drift off, Sutton's brain had practically gone bioluminescent with ideas for how to spend their days off between Christmas and New Year's Eve.

She reached for her phone to check the time. 9:17 a.m. So the day wasn't off to the start she'd planned. With Cami at Dolce, likely for the next couple of hours, she could get her workout in and probably make that perfumery class she'd been taking in an attempt to not fuck up the ambitious Christmas gift she had in mind. Except, the only sample—a lavender forward floral blend with musk and sandalwood base notes—she'd been bold enough to test, dabbing a hint of it behind her own ears, hadn't yielded any interest from Cami. It *was* possible she hadn't noticed, given Sutton had chosen the worst day to do a test run—the one Cami found out about Lupe and Martín's divorce, on top of an otherwise stressful workday.

She *could* wear it again, see if Cami said anything, but maybe, just maybe, Sutton had overestimated herself. Even after two months of biweekly classes, she didn't know anything about making perfumes. Chemists studied the art of blending scents for years, and she'd convinced herself she could do it in a couple of months.

Go fucking figure.

She gave the doubt free rein to swim through her brain for another fifteen seconds before forcing herself to her feet. Any longer and she'd think herself into paralysis, unable to commit to any one idea for hours on end, which would indubitably lead to another conversation on imposter syndrome with Dr. Copeland.

She shook her head, willing away the thought as she picked up her phone to tap out a reply to Cami.

POWDERED SUGAR DRIZZLED from Cami's fingers onto a gleaming batch of buñuelos as her phone lit up against the counter. Mami would kill her for even having it in sight when the bakery was this busy, but Mami wasn't here. Besides, even having not worked here since she was an undergrad trying to make up extra money during breaks, her body fed off the stream of orders like a shot of pure adrenaline. Figures Luci would end up short-staffed a week before Christmas, when people overcommitted and under-prepared.

After falling into bed, curling into Sutton's arms well after one a.m., Cami probably should've rolled over and gone back to sleep when she saw Luci calling at five, but she figured her sister was desperate. Besides, the whiny little voice in the back of her mind, otherwise called her conscience, wouldn't have let her sleep in peace if she hadn't picked up. And this was what she got for having scruples—spending Saturday morning at Dolce, instead of waking up well-rested next to the love of her life.

She brushed a hand against her apron and tapped her screen with one finger, angling her head for the face ID to initiate and give her a full view of the incoming texts.

SUTTON (9:26 A.M.)

Later, I'll have a few words for Luci about taking my wife out of bed on a Saturday morning to work somewhere she doesn't even work anymore. For now...

Have a good shift, baby. I love you.

PS. I missed the notes.

Cami nipped her bottom lip, resisting the urge to grin like a lovestruck teenager. She didn't know what it said about her that she loved when Sutton used the words *my wife*, that she loved the claim in it, the sense of belonging, even after three years of marriage. Thoughts of last night lingered in her mind though, the hours of music, decorating and kissing so difficult to reconcile with everything she'd been feeling over the last week, last few months, she couldn't begin to process it.

Last night, Sutton had promised her forever, and Cami had seen truth in her eyes, tasted it on her lips. But Cami still didn't know what to do with the rest of it—the "doctor's appointments" Sutton hadn't invited her to or even bothered to explain, her spasmodic irritability, that fucking perfume. It would've been easy to assume Sutton had just changed hers, but she'd worn the same vanilla rose scent since Luci had brought her home to visit when Cami was eighteen. Besides, Cami had checked their vanity—not that she was proud of it—and she didn't find anything to indicate that Sutton was trying a new scent.

"*No phones* in the kitchen," Luci scolded.

Cami rolled her eyes, but before she could turn and iterate how much her sister wasn't the boss of her—something she'd been asserting since they were five and ten, respectively—Luci sidled up next to her and peered down at her screen.

"Guessing last night went well then."

Cami clicked the lock screen button, glaring at her. "Que chismosa."

"Ay, por favor, Cami." Luci waved her off. "It's not like Sutton's not going to tell me everything anyway. I mean, not *everything*"—she scrunched up her face, waving a hand at Cami—"considering."

"I swear you forget which one of us is your sister."

"Nope. Because only one of you came wailing into the world wearing a carbon copy of my face after putting Mami through twenty-three hours of labor." Luci beamed, but Cami's thoughts were lagging, still stuck on the idea of Sutton telling Luci everything.

She understood the implication behind the addendum —she'd draw the line at detailed recounts of her sister's sex life too—but everything else... After a decade of friendship between them, there was no one Sutton trusted more.

Cami's brows twitched, and she dropped her gaze, unable to look at her sister directly when she said, "I know she's your best friend, but you would tell me, right? If something was wrong, if there was something to worry about."

"What?" Luci shook her head, her smile fading. "What happened last night?"

"Nothing. It was great. We hung the lights and laughed and kissed, and it was"—Cami sighed, glancing skyward—"perfect. She was perfect. She was... *Sutton*, you know? It just came at a really weird time, and I don't know. Something still feels off, and it's like you said, she tells you everything, because you're her best friend, but *I'm* your sister. I'm not asking you what it is. I'm saying you would tell me, right?"

"Cam..." Luci ducked her head, searching for Cami's gaze.

"We're low on atole!" Gigi, the cashier, called from the register, the lengthening line on the opposite end of the counter offering a vivid reminder that this was neither the time nor place to have this conversation.

"I'll get it." Cami started deeper into the kitchen, but Luci caught her arm, pulling until they were face to face again. "Luce, we don't have time—"

"Veinte segundos más no matarán a nadie," she whispered. "*Of course*, I'd tell you. No question. But Cam..." Her brows inched closer, and her lips parted then shut, almost as if she wasn't sure she wanted to say her next words. "Sutton's not Noa. I know you know that, but if you need your big sister to give your wife a figurative kick in the ass, I've got you."

Cami's lips quirked in a smile—goal accomplished, knowing Luci.

"I also know—"

"Buenas buenas!" Mami burst into the kitchen, stealing their attention, though Luci managed to shoot Cami a look that said their conversation wasn't over. Guadalupe Morales would never abide idle chatter while there were customers waiting, unless it was to catch up with each regular that crossed the counter. Cami could practically hear her already, the way her accent grew thicker whenever she had another Spanish speaker to confer with:

Karla, como estan las niñas? Y tu esposo?

Que bueno, que bueno...

Oye, viste que TJ Maxx esta en oferta?

Cami hurriedly crossed the tiled floors to peck her mom on the cheek, "Hola, Mami. Atole's low," before rushing toward the sink to wash her hands and check the stock pot.

A steaming gust of guava misted her vision as she swirled the contents with a ladle, and a knot twisted in her stomach, reminding her that she'd skipped breakfast. All this food around her and she'd barely downed three sips of coffee.

She grabbed a clean chafing dish and filled it with atole, then started toward the display counter to replace the empty one. Eyes trailed her the whole way there, but she'd adjusted to the remodel years ago—the open layout facilitating a more immersive experience where customers could see the staff at work. She'd learned to take pride in their fascination with the process and constant flow of fresh ingredients, while never sacrificing any of the care it took to get each pastry precise in size, shape, and décor. Even after trading her apron for a briefcase half a decade ago, the feeling hadn't waned.

Still, she almost wished she could get lost in it like she used to, in the exhaustion of being up since three a.m., in being up to her elbows in flour and spices for hours on end, never realizing how much her feet hurt until she finally sat down. But she couldn't. She was still stuck on the ambivalence of last night and Sutton's text and *missing something*.

Sutton's not Noa, Luci's voice echoed in her head.

Cami knew that. Of course she knew that, and maybe, that was why she couldn't bring herself to outright verbalize the gut-wrenching fear of losing Sutton to someone else. The very implication screamed accusation, and if it wasn't true—and it *couldn't* be—she didn't want to face the look in Sutton's eyes after letting holes left in her by the most unremarkable person she'd ever known warp her love of someone extraordinary.

Just as she was about to return to the buñuelos she'd been tending to earlier, a hand landed on her elbow, dragging her into the small break room off the side of the kitchen. "Ma? Qué paso?"

"What kind of cookies will you and Sutton be bringing for the contest?"

Cami didn't need much context to decipher that her mom meant the annual cookie-decorating contest they did every Nochebuena. That didn't stop her from squinting and tilting her head. "We're... bringing the cookies?"

"Pues, sí. We confirmed weeks ago."

"Weeks ago?" Cami uttered.

"Ay, Camila." Mami dug into her multi-print jacket and came out with her phone, her free hand reaching for the glasses she practically wore as a necklace, though she had a matching lanyard for every outfit. She swiped to Whatsapp, but instead of Cami's contact, she opened Sutton's, searching through a much longer chat than expected before angling the screen as proof. "November 29."

Warmth crept into Cami's chest as she read the exchange, all written in Spanish, though Sutton always got too anxious about her grammar.

Cami chuckled. "Mami, you do realize this only confirms you told Sutton, not me."

"Same difference. You two sleep in the same bed."

"Right." Cami wasn't sure her marriage followed that logic of late, but she wasn't about to dwell on it when her mom was the one getting a divorce, especially when everyone was determined to treat it as a nonevent. Business as usual. "Cookies, got it."

"And make extra reindeer," said Mami. "They're Sofi and Regi's favorite."

"I know, Ma. I'll talk to Sutton. We'll take care of it."

"Bueno." She clapped, already moving past Cami toward the kitchen. "Back to work, then."

Cami hung back, reaching for her phone at the memory that she still hadn't replied to her wife's earlier messages. "Yeah. I'll be out in five."

Mami aimed a stern finger at her. "No te tardes. We have customers."

Cami shook her head, incredulous, though this was entirely like her mom. "You and Luci do remember I don't work here anymore, right?"

"Ahh sí? Your Papi and I break our necks to send you to law school for all this back talk?" Mami glared at her, the look on her wizened, tawny face somehow as threatening as it was amusing. "As long as you're on this side of the counter, you're working, *y ya*."

Cami sputtered a laugh, holding up a hand, but before she could say another word Mami was stomping toward the door, leaving a trail of indignant mumbles in her wake.

Chapter 8

TEXTS WITH SUTTON

CAMI (9:41 A.M.)

Did you forget to mention something?

SUTTON (9:42 A.M.)

I… don't think so?

CAMI (9:42 A.M.)

When were you going to tell me we're making the noche cookies?

SUTTON (9:42 A.M.)

Fuck 🤦‍♀️

Babe, I'm so sorry.

Your mom messaged. You had a deposition, and I knew if I didn't say yes she'd just keep trying to call you. Must've spaced when I got home.

CAMI (9:43 A.M.)

It's okay.

Luckily, we still have a week to get everything we need.

SUTTON (9:43 A.M.)

A week? We have to practice.

And by that I mean not wait until the night before.

CAMI (9:44 A.M.)

Baby, I've been making these cookies since I was sixteen.

SUTTON (9:44 A.M.)

I haven't.

I want to help. Otherwise, you do all the work and we both take the credit.

How will I sleep at night?

CAMI (9:45 A.M.)

😌 Is there anything being cute hasn't gotten you?

SUTTON (9:45 A.M.)

Baby, being cute literally never served me a day in my life until I met you.

Probably because you're the only person who'd ever dare call me that.

CAMI (9:46 A.M.)

Not true, but I'll be more equipped to argue my point later.

Mami's on a warpath so I have to go.

I'll be home when the rush dies down.

SUTTON (9:47 A.M.)

Which is probably never, if it's anything like it usually is during the holidays.

How's salmon?

CAMI (9:47 A.M.)

Salmon?

SUTTON (9:47 A.M.)

For dinner.

Figure you'll probably be exhausted when you get home, so instead of suggesting we go out...

I'm going to cook.

CAMI (9:47 A.M.)

You're cooking?

SUTTON (9:47 A.M.)

Haha, yes?

I know it's been a minute, but we spend way too much money on takeout.

Besides, I'm on vacation in two days. Feels like the perfect time to pick up old habits.

CAMI (9:48 A.M.)

I could get on board with that.

PS. Salmon sounds perfect.

SUTTON (9:48 A.M.)

PS. I love you.

CAMI (9:48 A.M.)

I love you too.

Chapter 9

SMELLS LIKE TEEN SPIR—UH, CHRISTMAS

An upbeat rendition from Luis Miguel's *Navidades* flowed into the kitchen as Sutton lowered the haul of sugar, baking powder, and vanilla she'd grabbed from the pantry onto the island counter. Cami swayed to the beat, mumbling along with the lyrics, though her hands were already busy with a measuring cup teeming with flour and the large bowl underneath.

A fragrant medley of pine and menthol had altered the air since they'd laid out the tree and nochebuenas last Friday. And it never snowed in San Francisco—at least not that Sutton had seen—but the slight drop in temperature felt just on theme for December. God knows snow made a pretty picture, but she could always do without having to shovel inches of it off her front steps, only to minimize the risk of breaking her neck every time she dared to venture outside.

She sidled up behind Cami, the braided tresses dangling from her bun tickling Sutton's face when her chin found Cami's shoulder. Slipping one hand beneath Cami's tank top, if only for the rush, the warmth, of her skin against her palm, Sutton pulled Cami closer and peered down at the tattered pages of her family's recipe book. "Is that everything we need?"

"Think so." Cami turned in her arms, reluctant to pause her swaying, thereby leaving Sutton little choice but to smile and keep up. "We *should* probably put those away." She bobbed her head to the pair of old fashioned tumblers standing amidst the spread of baking ingredients. "But I'm guessing you left them out for a reason."

"I did..." Sutton drew out, beaming.

Cami's eyes rolled skyward. "You know we don't need a specialty drink for *every* occasion, right?"

"I mean, I know we don't *need* one, but..." Sutton held up a finger, backing away toward the fridge before swinging the door open and emerging with a pitcher filled with the latest concoction she'd swiped from the internet. "You only say that because you haven't tried this one."

Cami crossed both arms beneath her chest, brows arched though amusement blazed in her eyes. "So this is what you've been up to your first day on vacation?"

"Among other things." Sutton bobbed her head side to side as she filled both glasses. She could've mentioned how she hadn't been able to sleep in like she'd planned, or how she'd checked her email twice under the guise of making sure she hadn't forgotten to set her out-of-office message, never mind a third time just in case of any director-specific emergencies. Dr. Copeland's insistent scribbling during her therapy session suggested the woman didn't exactly approve, but this was Sutton's first vacation in a year. Remembering *how* to vacation was... a work in progress.

Besides, Copeland seemed well on board with Sutton taking her suggestion to plan a night with Cami and evolving it into a slew of other ideas for the holidays. Pomegranate gin fizz cocktails as an accompaniment to baking practice was merely one of them.

She handed Cami a glass, watching over the rim of her tumbler as they both sipped.

Cami pulled the drink away to blink at it then stared at Sutton wide-eyed. "Okay, wow."

"Right?" Sutton swiped a lingering taste from her own lips.

A grin slipped onto Cami's face as she leaned closer, lips cold with the slightest tinge of red as she wordlessly followed up where Sutton's tongue left off, stirring that insistent little flutter in her chest, and making her skin heat. Then she pulled away, just enough for their eyes to lock. "A little strong though. I should probably take it slow. You know, in the interest of not fucking up the measurements and burning the cookies."

"I may have overdone the gin." Their fingers brushed as she reached for Cami's drink and placed both glasses on the counter. "Slow sounds like a good idea."

"Then again, I *have* done this enough times to bake these in my sleep," said Cami.

"Eh. Sounds like a fire hazard." Sutton scrunched up her face, bopping Cami on the tip of her nose before turning to survey the ingredients again. If anything, her sensitivity to Cami's touch, to kisses that deftly straddled the line between chaste and provocative, was a smoking gun. If they didn't start baking now, her hands would soon find themselves otherwise occupied. "So, where do you want me?"

"I can think of a few places." Cami grinned.

Sutton held up a finger. "*Not* what I meant."

"It's what you said. I don't know, babe. Might want to check in with your subconscious."

"Fine," said Sutton through a laugh, purposely enunciating her next words. "*How do I help*?"

"Grab the butter and sugar and follow these instructions." Cami tapped the page. "But since this is practice, we'll only use a third of the quantities there."

"Or we could do them all and I drop some off at the shelter tomorrow."

Cami tilted her head. "Really?"

Sutton shrugged. "I'm free all day, and everyone deserves delicious desserts for Christmas."

Cami's expression softened, her eye contact never waning, her grin growing even more dopey as she swept her thumb over Sutton's cheek. "I think that's a great idea."

Sutton's brows twitched in confusion. She didn't think doing something Luci and Lupe did almost daily, sending baked goods to several shelters across the Mission and South of Market, deserved Cami looking at her like she'd brought water from the moon. But before she could decide how to address it, Cami redirected to the counter and grabbed the flour bag. Reaching for the sugar and butter, Sutton undertook her own task of adding them to the mixing bowl and beating them with the mixer as instructed. Not that she was exactly clear on what *until creamy* meant. Because, clearly, a precise length of time was too much to ask for.

The current song on their playlist hit the bridge and Cami joined in, using the metal whisk for a microphone as she belted the lyrics through to the end, then picked up cracking the eggs one after the other without missing a beat. By the time her gaze flicked up, a smile ghosting her mouth despite her furrowed brows, Sutton had lost track of how long she'd even been staring. "What?"

"Nothing." Sutton shook her head, her heart racing at

the mere existence of this person she got to fall asleep next to every night. "I just... I think a part of me always wondered why you didn't co-manage Dolce with Luci. I mean, I know *why* you went into family law, but I guess you'd probably have more peaceful days than at Dimaano."

Cami shrugged. "I don't think either of us picked our careers on the basis of them being peaceful. Besides, it's different doing something you love for the joy of it, instead of because it's your job. Managing Dolce... it's not just baking. There's staff and inventory and supplier lists. Luce thrives on that stuff, even if she's constantly on the verge of losing her mind with it all. Plus"—she paused, drying her hands on a towel as she moved toward Sutton—"I don't ever want to get used to leaving our bed, leaving you, at three a.m. every morning."

Sutton's eyes trailed each step until Cami stopped in front of her, close enough that the steady rise and fall of their chests left them touching. "Yeah, I'd probably hate that."

Cami reached for her glass and took another sip, her tongue darting out to rid her top lip of the foam left behind, much like Sutton had done earlier. "Probably?"

"Definitely." Sutton nodded, the hairs on the back of her neck rising. "Like, right up there with baby-kissing politicians."

A breathy chuckle drifted between them as Cami lowered her glass and leaned in.

"I thought we were baking," said Sutton.

"What? The practice cookies you insisted we make on a random Wednesday night, which have the extensive baking time of a whopping ten minutes? I think they'll be fine." Cami paused, her eyes trained on Sutton's mouth. "Besides,

I'm not sure how you expect me to focus when you keep staring at me like I'm slathered in icing."

Words clamored for purchase in Sutton's brain, something soft and witty on the tip of her tongue about how tonight wasn't random, or about the cookies. Maybe the Sutton who'd been raised on *do it right or not at all* would refuse to show up on her mother-in-law's doorstep with anything but a flawless spread of vanilla-flavored reindeer, pine trees, and gingerbread men, but it's not like her wife's family of bakers would think she had much to do with it.

Baking was Cami's domain, and there was something about watching her work—the serenity of flour streaks on her face, eyes gleaming as she hummed and rocked to the music—that left Sutton weightless, awestruck, every single time.

Their lips touched, Cami's palms tracing the sleeves of Sutton's sweatshirt, then lower, slipping beneath the hem and leaving Sutton's semi-exposed abdomen taut at the very brush of her fingers. Sutton's eyes fell shut, and she gripped the edge of the counter, despite the marble biting into her back. "We both know if you kiss me right now, those cookies are never making it to the oven."

"Consider it a calculated risk." Cami's lips pillowed against hers, sweet and tart with traces of pomegranate. The corners of her mouth ticked up in a smile Sutton felt more than saw, but within seconds they were kissing again. Slow, indulgent, coiling the knot beneath Sutton's navel tighter and tighter.

She cupped Cami's face, swiping her tongue against her bottom lip, sighing when Cami opened her mouth wider and tilted her head to deepen the kiss. Blunt nails dragged along Sutton's sides, finding the hem of her sweater and tugging it over her head. Her heart raced, leaving her hands shaky with the mounting tension, with the need to feel Cami's skin on hers, so she reached for Cami's tank top and yanked it off too.

Months. How had they gone months without doing this? For what? Late nights spent slaving over contracts, angling for an accomplishment that felt hollow in the aftermath, that definitely didn't, *couldn't* compare to—

Cami's hands drifted to Sutton's outer thighs, a maneuver she'd experienced countless moments before being hoisted onto a counter or table, their bathroom vanity. Her grip tightened but she paused, Sutton following as her eyes darted to the counter behind them. Far be it from Sutton to yuck anyone's yum, but finding herself splattered in eggs and butter with her wife knuckle deep inside her didn't make her fantasy top five.

"Bed?" Cami panted.

Sutton shook her head. "Too far." She flattened a palm against Cami's abdomen, guiding her back against the adjacent wall with a muffled thud. A thunk echoed against the floor, followed by the clatter of keys, but Sutton's hands were already sweeping up Cami's softened curves and belly to cup her breasts. Her nipples pebbled against the thin cotton of her bra, beckoning for the pads of Sutton's thumbs.

Cami gasped, pulling away just long enough to murmur, "I missed you. I missed you *like this.*" One hand swept up, threading through Sutton's hair and holding her close as her lips found Cami's pulse point.

She kissed a trail along the hinge of Cami's jaw to the small gold ring adorning her ear, and rolled both nipples between her fingers, gently, then harder.

"Fuck, Sutton."

Just hard enough to make Cami whine her name like *that.* A hundred images rippled through her mind. Visions of them stumbling across the living room to the couch, leaving a trail of crooked frames and tumbled furniture in their wake, the look in Cami's eyes when she inevitably shoved Sutton onto the couch, straddled her, and sunk onto her fingers. The way she'd drop her head back and groan, swearing and pleading with every thrust.

There was also something about having her against their kitchen wall, nothing but the weight of Sutton's body to prop her up, that had Sutton aching with the need to strip her bare and take her to pieces right here. She yanked at the strings of Cami's fluffy lounge pants, unraveling the knot and pushing them down her thighs as she dropped to her knees. "I need my mouth on you."

"Yes. Please, yes."

The heat creeping through Sutton's body, never mind the throbbing between her thighs said she was much too far gone for slow. But the sight of Cami standing above her, legs spread and waiting shattered their frantic pace, replacing it with a reverence that had Sutton raking her hair back—the curls wild from having Cami's fingers in them mere seconds ago. She sat back on her heels, trailing one hand up the inside of Cami's thigh to the seam of her underwear, to the faintest glimmer of arousal darkening the plum-colored fabric.

Cami dropped her head back against the wall. "No teasing."

"Are you asking?" Sutton dragged her thumb up, then paused, tracing featherlight arcs against Cami's clit over her panties. "Or telling?"

"You can take as much time with me as you want later. Right now, I just need... I just—*Fuck*." Her knees buckled slightly.

"I've got you." Sutton steadied her with both hands on

her thighs, confirming her gaze, the enthusiastic nod, before tugging her underwear down and leaving them at her feet. One hand trailed her outer thigh, hoisting her left leg onto Sutton's shoulder, reveling in the anticipatory moan when Sutton dragged the tip of her nose through the dark curls covering her mound and hummed.

Cami's hand dropped to her head, leading as she shifted her hips to align with Sutton's mouth. Any other time, Sutton might've dragged it out, made her wait, made her beg. Tonight, she was powerless to do anything but let Cami guide her, to do anything but lean in and drag her tongue from her core to her clit.

"*Oh my God.*" Cami's grip on her hair tightened, tugging just enough to make stars flash behind Sutton's closed eyes.

She lapped at her gently anyway, licking and sucking and reveling in the taste of her. Cami mumbled her name, and her eyes darted open, the mere utterance like a jolt to her subconscious, reminding her she never ever wanted to miss a second of the pleasure unraveling on Cami's face. Shimmering brown eyes locked on Sutton as she nipped her bottom lip, fingers twisting her own nipples. There was still one thing that always left her a gorgeous, babbling mess.

Both hands planted on her inner thighs, Sutton slid her tongue lower, circling her entrance. Cami's moans grew pitchier and her eyes fell shut as her hand dropped to her hip, inching toward her clit.

"Don't you dare," Sutton mumbled, breathless, aching. There were few things that riled her up more than watching Cami touch herself. Having Cami this on edge, this desperate and out of control, pleading for Sutton to *give* her the orgasm they both craved more than air, was one of them.

"Fuck, Sutton, *please*. I'm so close." Her hand shifted lower, cupping Sutton's jaw. "I'm so fucking close, baby."

There were lots of things Sutton couldn't reconcile. The size or complete non-existence of pockets on women's pants. Menus without prices. Why traffic lights weren't better synchronized during fucking rush hour. Top of the list: her desire to keep Cami on the edge for as long as possible then feel compelled to give her whatever she wanted the second she whimpered, *baby*.

Sutton wrapped her lips around her clit and slipped two fingers inside, crooking them against that one spot that made Cami's legs tremor.

A guttural cry echoed off the walls, and she descended to mumbles, a melody of *yes, please, baby*, clenching around Sutton's fingers as she came.

Sutton didn't let up, even as she extracted herself from between Cami's thighs in a desperate quest for air, lips and chin drenched in arousal when she scrambled to her feet. It was almost, almost, like the very first night, how they'd barely made it through the door of Sutton's loft before Cami's hands were on her—all craving and lust. Their mouths found each other in a messy waltz of tongue and teeth, Cami's nails digging into Sutton's wrist as she curled inside her again, thumb dragging over her clit.

"Don't stop. Please don't stop."

"Stop?" Sutton chuckled, her breaths labored. If there was one thing five years of *slower, harder, just like that* had taught her, it was exactly when *not* to stop. She detached Cami's hand from her wrist, intertwining their fingers as she pinned it to the smooth, cool surface of the wall. Heat pooled along her spine and a faint ache pulsed in her wrist, but she increased her pace, the sound of her fingers driving deeper an almost obscene base note to Cami's whimpers. "I won't." She shook her head, whispering the words into Cami's mouth. "I won't stop until you're dripping down my hand and my name's the only thing you can taste. Until you're so tight I can barely—"

Cami gasped and her hips bucked as she clenched around Sutton's fingers, her body trembling. She swallowed hard. "Sutton, baby, I—"

"That's it. Let go." Even with the sharp burst of pain darting up her spine, Cami's grip tight, biting, the transition from tensing muscles and scrunched up ecstasy on Cami's face to the post-orgasmic bliss of her loosening in Sutton's arms always felt like Sutton catching her breath after being under water for too long.

Maybe it was the relief of knowing she could still unravel Cami this way, leave her glossy-eyed, messy, and so exquisitely beautiful, even while dancing the line of trying to recover everything she'd let fade to the background. Things like the simplicity of tree decorating, and Saturday nights with home-cooked dinners on the couch, ignoring the TV while Cami recounted her day at Dolce. And this... a form of intimacy that had always been so intrinsic to their relationship, that had come almost too easily from day one.

Sutton slowly slipped her fingers out, mapping an erotic trail along Cami's inner thigh straight to her hip, and Cami's eyes fluttered open with a groan. Their mouths brushed, the frenzied tousle of lips and tongues having quelled to a sweeter, more exploratory kiss, so indulgent Sutton released Cami's pinned hand, delighting in the sweep of those same fingertips along her nape. Sweet, like pomegranate and gin, heightened by the taste of Cami on Sutton's tongue.

Cami broke the kiss with a breathy chuckle. "I don't think I can feel my legs."

A laugh swelled in Sutton's chest, but she circled Cami's waist with both arms, brushing the bridge of her nose along the hinge of Cami's jaw. "This will probably sound self-aggrandizing, but I think that's normal after coming the way you just did."

"Still amazes me how you swear like a sailor but slip words like aggrandizing into post-sex banter."

"I could point you to several studies about the relationship between cursing and intelligence, but the truth is I kind of just like the word fuck. Partial to it as a verb, actually." Sutton grinned. "Besides, you're the lawyer."

"*Shh.*" Cami shook her head, warm hands emerging beneath Sutton's breasts, making her gasp at the gentle squeeze. "I don't want to debate vocabularies."

"I'd ask what you do want, but I get the feeling you're about to show me."

Cami dipped her head, leaving a trail of open-mouthed kisses along Sutton's neck, her chin, the sharp curve of her jaw, to the spot just beneath her ear lobe. "Put your hands on the counter."

"What?" Sutton blinked, despite the intensifying throbbing between her thighs, desire scorching through every inch of her. She understood the words, in theory. She'd said them to Cami more times than she could remember, but being on the receiving end...

A roguish smirk slinked onto Cami's face, and she turned Sutton in the intended direction, toward the slew of baking ingredients arranged across the counter. One hand swept the hair off Sutton's shoulder, the brush of fingers swiftly replaced by Cami's mouth along the column of her neck.

"Cami." Sutton's eyes drifted shut as she latched on to cold marble, slumping into the warmth, the sheer eroticism of Cami's breasts against her bare back, never mind the arm slinking around her to tweak her nipple while the other curved around her waist and into her shorts. Two fingers circled her clit, sliding between her folds, leaving zero doubt about how acutely wet she was, only to apply the slightest pressure to her entrance. "*Fuck*."

"Yeah?"

"Yes." Sutton nodded, reaching one arm back to loop around Cami's neck, needing her closer, needing her *now*.

"Hand. On. The. Counter," said Cami, her tone firm.

Sutton would've argued. She *wanted* to argue. Except, the fingers between her thighs had gone completely still, and something told her the pleasure rising and cresting beneath her navel would remain just out of reach until she complied. Chest heaving, toes curled against hardwood, she reluctantly gripped the counter with both hands and waited.

"Good." Cami's teeth grazed the delicate arch where her neck met her shoulder. "This time... don't let go."

Chapter 10

NOCHEBUENA

Brisk afternoon winds swept through the street, rustling the leaves of the towering Ficus that stood on the curb outside the townhouse Cami's parents had shared almost all her life. Despite her initial spiral after finding out about the divorce, she was grateful its faded gray paint and paneled walls would always be here, grateful for not having to contemplate what she'd do with the mile-high stack of boxes still housing childhood pictures and trophies in the basement. Her parents had always been too sentimental to throw away anything of perceived value, so this —*home*—she knew was here to stay.

She hit a button on her key fob and stepped away from the car as the trunk descended, looking up to find that Sutton was already halfway to the front door. "You know we're already late, right?" she called, wrangling a horde of gift, food, and wine bags between both hands.

Sutton glared over her shoulder, the three boxes of cookies they'd baked this morning precariously stacked in her grip. "Well, I'm not speedwalking for fun, babe."

"I meant ten more seconds won't make a difference."

"Sure. I'll let *you* explain that to your mom."

Cami chuckled, boots tapping against the concrete in a dance between a power walk and a brief jog. "Okay, but wait for a second."

Sutton paused by the door, her brows dipped in confusion, though her apprehension probably outweighed it. A decade and she still got nervous every time she was about to be under the same roof with Cami's family, even though they'd only been in a relationship the last five. Her gaze flitted to the car. "Did we leave something?"

"No. Just... here." Cami shifted all the bags to one hand, biting down on a smile as she plucked nonexistent lint from Sutton's shirt. A distraction. A wordless reminder for her to stop for a second. *Breathe*. The pop of red along her neckline, placket, and cuffs combined with the chiffon fabric was as much of a festive twist as Sutton ever added to her wardrobe, but as Cami adjusted the collar to conceal the darkening hickey at her pulse point, she'd never been more grateful for her wife's affinity for literally being too buttoned up.

Like clockwork, a montage of their most recent trysts darted through Cami's mind. Three nights ago in the kitchen, Sutton's pale-knuckled grip on the counter as Cami's fingers worked her closer to release, the way she pleaded and whined like she'd never done, only to pay it back tenfold the morning after. Already on vacation, she'd slipped into their closet, watching Cami get dressed before sidling up behind her as she checked her reflection in the full-length mirror. The vision of Sutton's hand disappearing beneath her skirt, shifting her panties aside, the fabric biting into the crease of her thigh combined with the knee-buckling pleasure of soft circles on her clit, had haunted Cami well into the work day, leaving her so distracted Justin had asked not twice but three times if she was feeling okay.

She couldn't pinpoint when the reset had happened, or why. She couldn't explain the sweeping shift from months of kisses that always ended with the abruptness of one of them having somewhere else to be, a meeting to prep for or calls to take, to the primal rush of hardly being able to keep their hands off each other now.

"Stop," said Sutton, her voice soft with warning when she cupped Cami's hand and pulled it away from her collar. Something familiar flashed in her eyes, something that said she knew exactly what Cami was feeling, the flicker of embers warming her from the inside out. "You can't look at me like that. Not now. Definitely not *here*."

Cami moved closer, mischief flirting with the corners of her mouth. "Like what?"

"*Camila...*"

"I don't think saying my name with that edge in your tone is helping either of us."

"You're impossible," Sutton gritted out, a smile breaking through. "We're literally outside your parents' house, and I can't have anything but holy thoughts when I kiss them hello."

"Babe, don't you think it's time you put the hope that they don't know you've seen me naked to rest?"

"I refuse. I should also mention that naked isn't on the Nochebuena list of sanctioned words today."

"The *what*?" Cami sputtered a laugh, but before she could root further into her wife being the most ridiculous person alive, the front door swung open, carrying with it the scent of barbecued meat and other Morales delicacies, never mind the cacophony of loud conversation over Christmas songs streaming from the stereo. A pair of euphoric squeals followed, barely giving Cami or Sutton time to adjust before Sofia and Regina barreled into them, each set of tiny arms wrapping around a pair of legs before the girls made the coordinated decision to swap places.

Luci beamed, watching the whole exchange as her daughters trained big hazel eyes up at Cami and Sutton.

"Mami says you're late," said Sofi.

"I bet she did." Sutton unceremoniously shoved the cookies in Luci's direction, freeing her hands to pick up Regi. With only a year between her and Sofia, most days they could pass for twins, but Sofi, unlike Regi, had stopped wanting to be picked up the day she blew out her fifth birthday candles. After all, she *was* a big kid now.

"Hi, you." Sutton pressed a kiss to Regi's cheek, her other hand ruffling Sofi's hair. "Take care of the cookies," she aimed at Luci, already pushing past her and into the house, Regi in one arm as Sofi latched onto the other. "We have catching up to do, don't we?"

"Tía, did you bring us presents?"

"Did I bring you—" Sutton glanced between both girls, eyes widened in mock incredulity. "Of course, I brought you presents. You get all the presents, as long as you share with your brother."

Cami's heart swelled as she watched the exchange, their voices trailing off the farther they went into the house, though they only made it halfway through the living room before Papi swept in to plant a kiss on Sutton's cheek.

Luci's breathy chuckle drew Cami back. "It's a real-life miracle neither of you are pregnant yet with how obsessed she is with those kids."

Cami stepped inside, closing the door behind her. "Yeah, well, we both know it's different when you can't just give them back to their parents after."

"Don't I know it," said Luci. "But you do still want to, right? Have kids."

"Yeah. It just hasn't come up recently. We still have a lot to talk about. Guess we're waiting 'til the dust settles."

Luci's brows inched up. "That mark on Sutton's neck is definitely giving me settled."

Cami's head snapped in Sutton's direction, to where she stood talking to Papi and Luci's husband, Chema, only now with Regi tugging at the shirt collar Cami had taken great care to adjust mere minutes ago. Feigning nonchalance, Cami shrugged, ignoring her sister's probing stare in favor of scanning the kitchen for a spot to unload her bags. "It's a bee sting."

"Who has a bee sting?" The heavily accented inquiry gave away Mami's presence before she emerged from behind Cami, festively garbed in a red and white jacquard knit sweater and seamless pants.

A shit-eating grin crept onto Luci's face. "Sutton, apparently."

Mami glanced toward Sutton before facing Cami with a tired expression. "Mija, if your sister wants to pretend she was born yesterday, that is between the two of you and Dios." She pointed, actually fucking pointed at Sutton, in case any of the dozen other people in the living room needed context. "That is no bee sting. Next time, ten cuidado."

Cami cringed. "Ma—"

"We all get caught up in the passion sometimes."

"Mami, por favor, ya!"

A snicker escaped Luci.

"I don't know what you find so funny. Nobody thinks your three were inmaculada concepción."

"Yeah, no, we should definitely stop this," Luci grumbled, then thrust the boxes toward their mom. "Cookies are here."

Mami hmphed, but her gaze swept around the kitchen. Between the cling-wrapped dishes of pasta, salads, and chafing dishes filled with warmer foods taking up most of the counter, there was no space for the cookie boxes. "Come." She started into the living room, gesturing for them to follow. "We're running late for the contest anyway."

Cami bobbed her head for Luci to go ahead, only for her sister to glare in return. "I have to put away the ice cream and wine, then find room for everything else. Alone," she added with a chuckle. "I do love my nieces, but thanks to them, my wife is now too distracted to remember she has a wife."

Needless to say, the fridge was teeming with more drinks and desserts than the entire family could possibly consume, even considering everyone going home with filled-to-the-brim Tupperware. Fifteen minutes into a reorganization project that took twice as long with Cami's dad, then cousin Letty coming over with her son, Santiago, and a neighbor who'd planned on spending Christmas alone, Tía Celia called out that it was time for the cookie-decorating contest.

Cami abandoned her reshuffle to join everyone in the living room, where Mami stood at the center, hands raised like an orchestra director.

"Kids, on this side." She pointed to the craft table she and Papi had bought for anything ranging from weekend visits to larger family events, before turning to the coffee table a few inches away. No less than six reusable piping bags, each filled with a different color of icing, occupied the center of each table, while unadorned vanilla cookies—pine trees, reindeer, or the standard gingerbread man—awaited each contestant. "Adults, here. You know the rules. You all get one minute with each piping bag. No cheating. I'm talking to you Sofi."

Sofia snickered at the finger aimed at her, dark curls falling into her eyes as she shook her head. "No, 'buela."

"And you..." Mami swung her finger toward the adult table, only to lightly smack herself on the forehead. "Ay, pues. No Brady and Justin this year."

A laugh escaped Cami's lips, and she turned to give Sutton a knowing look. This year, Justin and Brady were with Brady's family in LA, but no one could forget their failed conspiracy to hide their table's bags of red and black icing in an effort to not run out of either color before finishing the matching tuxedos they'd decided for their reindeer cookies.

If Sutton's lack of response was anything to go by, eyes glued to her phone, thumbs tapping against the screen, she'd been too distracted to catch the reference.

Cami frowned, but redirected her attention to her mom as she continued summarizing the rules.

"Lucia, Cami, and I will be judging, and Celia and Martín will referee so there's no monkey business," Mami explained. "Don't try to make your gingerbread man look like me. It won't earn you extra points. In fact, it will cost you many. That one was for you, Jose Maria."

At that, Sutton did look up from her phone briefly enough to laugh at Chema.

"You have fifteen minutes," said Mami, whistle halfway to her mouth.

"Espera, espera!" Chema held up a palm, then plucked a purple hair tie—no doubt Sofi or Regi's—from his wrist to sweep his mid-length blond hair out of his face, his alabaster skin flushed with excitement.

Mami's eye roll would've done any teenager proud, but

Luci just beamed like she'd never been more in love with him.

The shriek of the whistle brought a frenzy of hands scrambling for the bags of red and white icing at the adult table. Meanwhile, over on the kids' side, Regi and Pablo already had mouths full of cookies, leaving Sofi and Santiago with the pick of mini piping bags to themselves. Sutton outlined one large eye on her cookie, then reached for the black icing to add three strokes next to it that left her reindeer looking like it was winking, all while she and Chema tousled shoulder to shoulder in a mutual act of subterfuge designed to throw off the other.

The family had long decided that neither Cami, Luci nor their parents should compete with everyone else, given all the years they'd spent baking professionally. They'd even devised a biennial All Star contest as a compromise, but not a single year had gone by that Cami didn't wish she was right there next to Sutton conferring over silly decorating ideas, instead of trying to remain objective.

As if she could sense Cami standing over her shoulder, Sutton glanced back, her entire face aglow with excitement as she shot Cami an exaggerated wink, much like the one she was attempting to craft for her reindeer.

Chema nudged her with his arm. "Ah ah! No seducing the judges."

Across the table, Letty and her neighbor laughed as Letty mumbled in Spanish that the contest was rigged. Not that either of them actually had to worry.

Cami had taken one look at Sutton and leaped off a figurative cliff for many a reason. The unparalleled radiance of her smile, though pictures of fifteen-year-old Sutton beaming through a mouthful of braces would forever hold a place in her heart. The reservation that had drawn her in almost as easily as Sutton's charm, even if it had taken years to crack the shield. She'd fallen for her beauty and brilliance, even the power in her stride that shrouded the absolute cinnamon roll of a person she was beneath it all.

Cami could fill encyclopedia volumes with all the things she loved about her wife. That Sutton happened to be the most adorably artistically challenged person she knew was one of them.

An insistent buzzing drew her gaze to Sutton's phone on the coffee table, the screen aglow with an unidentified number. Sutton glanced at it, then went back to her cookie before doing a double take and swiping up the phone instead. She bit down on her bottom lip, considering, but ultimately pushed herself to her feet and turned to Cami. "I have to take this."

Cami's eyes darted around the room to find Luci, Mami, and Papi already watching, though they averted their eyes the second Cami noticed. Luckily, everyone else was still too occupied with the contest. Taking Sutton's arm, Cami sighed, pulling her toward the kitchen. "Please tell me you're not working on Christmas."

"What? No. Of course not." Her gaze dropped to her still buzzing phone. "But I really do have to take this."

"Five more minutes!" Mami yelled.

"Actually, it's a little loud down here with the music and everything. I'll be right back." She whirled in the opposite direction, heading for the stairs without a glance back.

Cami drew in a breath, rubbing her forehead. "It's probably nothing," she mumbled to herself. *It* is *nothing*. Just Sutton being weird and insular like she'd been when they'd first met, but they were going to talk about it. She promised they'd talk about it.

Instead of letting her mind run wild with her worst

fears, Cami headed toward the living room, offering herself the distraction of Pablo's babbling and Chema's panicked efforts to shade in a beard on his gingerbread man before time ran out.

It was another two minutes before the thud of boots on the stairs alerted Cami to Sutton's return, and Cami retreated to meet her on the landing, concern thrumming through tensing muscles. "Everything okay?"

"Everything's perfect. Just something I needed to take care of." Sutton's lips stretched in an unrestrained smile that both warmed Cami and made her queasy, especially when hands cupped her cheeks and Sutton's lips claimed hers in a tender kiss. She pulled away, still grinning as she bobbed her head toward the living room. "Gonna see if I can finish my cookie."

With only two minutes left on the clock, she couldn't possibly get it done, but she took the loss in stride, cheering and clapping when Mami declared Letty's intricate gingerbread house, adorned with windows, a door, fairy lights and all, the winner. Sofi's festive pine tree took the medal for the kids, which Cami was sure her parents would be hearing about for the next year, but Cami clung to her niece's infectious energy, greeting her with a drawn out, "Wooow" when Sofi ran over to show her and Sutton the store-bought medal dangling from her neck.

By the time dinner had been served, a cloud of nostalgia had swept in, resulting in a ping pong of vibrant laughter and stories being traded across the table. That one time Luci had gotten drunk with older cousins on her first trip to Mexico City and almost got arrested over an open can of hard seltzer in Jardín del Arte. Or the one where Mami tried to throw Papi a surprise party for his fiftieth birthday and inadvertently included him in the group where she'd sent her two-paragraph text, warning everyone to be on time. Papi, being Papi, had been the first to reply: *No te preocupes, mi amor. I'll be there.*

Luci shook her head, smiling, though longing flickered in her eyes. "I can't believe you two are actually going through with it. The divorce."

Papi took Mami's hand, squeezing before pressing a kiss to her knuckles. Crows' feet creased the corners of his eyes, his ochre skin wizened with the years, hair the perfect blend of salt and pepper these days. "Your mother will always be the greatest love of my life, but it's what's best for both of us."

"We still have so much life to live," Mami joined in, though her eyes never left his. "This is how we let each other do that."

The shift in collective temper hit Cami like a sucker punch, though half the table took on wistful smiles as they nodded their understanding. Watching her parents, it felt like an unspoken agreement had passed between them even now—like those moments when Cami had been fifteen, sixteen, pleading to go to the kind of high school party her Mexican mother and Panamanian father always viewed with too much skepticism. But Cami knew better. Clearly, they'd been considering the divorce for a while.

Sutton leaned in to kiss her temple, the arm stretched across the back of Cami's chair squeezing her bicep in unison. "That's really beautiful, the way they put it."

Cami's eyes burned, her chest and throat tight with ambivalence. Maybe Sutton was right. Maybe there *was* beauty in letting go. Nothing made Cami happier than knowing her parents still saw a lifetime ahead of them, even as they were heading into their sixties. God knows Cami couldn't bear any less than three more decades of Papi's conspiracies that Juan Gabriel was definitely still alive, never mind Mami's filter-less commentary on her and Luci's lives. But there was something about Sutton's lack of conflict that wound a knot in Cami's belly so tight she had to press a hand to her stomach to stanch the nausea.

Nearly every second of the last two weeks dictated that she and Sutton weren't her parents, that their marriage wasn't anywhere close to divorce filings. And yet, two weeks ago, Cami would've sworn there was nothing her parents wanted as much as to be by each other's sides until the end of time. So clearly, she had her blind spots.

"Besides"—Papi waved a hand toward Cami and Sutton, Luci and Chema—"we have new generations of love stories to admire."

Mami held up a finger. "And make more nietos."

"She's talking to you two," said Luci, brows raised, a fork full of potato salad halfway to her mouth. She hooked a thumb toward Chema with her free hand. "After three kids in five years, we're wrapping it up. Literally."

Laughter rumbled through the room.

"Don't worry, Luce." Sutton gave her a playful nudge. "We'll tag you out. A couple of Christmases from now Pablo might not be the littlest one running around here. Right, babe?" She turned to Cami, cheery and expectant.

Papi oohed and Mami's eyes grew so bright, they rivaled the lights beaming from the Christmas tree towering toward the high ceiling.

Cami stared at Sutton, scrutinizing every inch of her gorgeous face. The glint in her eyes and quirk of her lips. Smooth slope of her cheeks and cut of her jaw. The radiance of her skin forever gleaming with reddish brown undertones. Cami had never doubted whether she would happily raise a dozen tiny humans with those features, never mind Sutton's heart of gold. She'd never doubted it, but suddenly her ribs felt painfully tight, her thoughts an impenetrable jumble with the typhoon of unanswered questions ripping through her brain.

Doctors' appointments. Cryptic texts and calls she hadn't even attempted to explain. Lavender perfume.

Cam... Sutton's not Noa, Luci's voice echoed.

A hand landed on Cami's cheek, drawing her back. "Babe?"

She blinked, clearing her throat. "Yeah. Sorry."

Sutton tilted her head, her gaze steady with concern, and Cami could sense the question about to roll off her tongue. *Are you okay? What's wrong?* But Cami didn't know what she'd say, because *no*, she wasn't okay. And she couldn't do this here, with her parents and sister and everyone watching them.

She'd told Sutton that she didn't need to know what lay behind the months-long falter in their work/life balance, behind Sutton pulling away only to show up like nothing significant had happened. Baking and decorating and having dinner ready before Cami even made it through the door nearly every day of the last week. The way she touched Cami, kissed her with everything from unbearable tenderness to searing passion...

But Cami *did* need to know. She didn't see how she'd get past this otherwise.

Were they really okay, or was everything Sutton had been doing an elaborate band-aid to an ailment that ran much deeper?

Chapter 11

LAVENDER HAZE

The door clicked shut behind Sutton as she trailed Cami into their apartment, a bag brimming with leftovers in one hand, car keys in the other. It was impossible to miss the gradual change in Cami's mood as the day stretched on, the buoyant flirtation of this afternoon long replaced by cautious looks and Cami completely zoning out at dinner. Talk of Lupe and Martín's divorce had seemed the most likely explanation, but she'd barely said a word to Sutton in the hours after—not during dessert, or through the hilarity of Christmas karaoke, definitely not on the drive home.

Sutton offloaded the bag onto their kitchen counter and dropped the keys in the assigned tray, turning to Cami, who'd yet to even look at her. "Cam."

As if that single utterance of her name was all she needed, Cami whirled in Sutton's direction. Braided tresses framed her face on either side, the rest still wrapped in the intricate bun she'd spent twenty minutes on this morning, and the faintest tinge of red had crept up the column of her neck, flaring from beneath her bubblegum turtleneck and onto her cheeks. Sutton itched to move closer, but something told her that wasn't what Cami wanted. Not right now.

"What are we doing, Sutton?"

"I don't..." Sutton paused, wincing as she considered the question. "I don't know what that means." The last time those words had left Cami's lips with this much force, they'd been secretly dating for two months—Sutton winding herself in circles over how to tell Luci, Cami insisting that they didn't need anyone's permission. Not that it had ever been about approval for Sutton, so much as the cloak-and-dagger of it all. Falling in love with her best friend's younger sister felt like an unspoken rule she'd shattered. Unavoidable, perhaps even inevitable. A breach of trust, nonetheless. They were so far beyond that now, but at least then, Sutton knew why Cami had been fuming, disappointed.

"What was that at dinner?" Cami asked, her tone sharp, expression pinched. "Promising them grandkids?"

So this was about the—

Sutton shook her head, blinking. "Isn't that what we always talked about? I'll carry when I'm thirty-three, then you two years after."

"Do you seriously think we're in a place to be having kids right now?"

"Well, it's not a piece of toast, Cam. It's not like we'll slide them in there and they'll pop out in two minutes."

Cami scoffed, glaring. "Very funny, Sutton."

"What? What is this really about? If it's not what you want anymore—"

"Not what I want?" Cami flinched, eyes wide, incredulous. "Sutton, what I want is to know what the fuck has been going on with you."

"Okay." Sutton nodded, drawing in a steadying breath as she gave in to the urge to move closer. There were things she hadn't said, things she'd promised to explain, had maybe glossed over in the last few weeks. If she was being honest, there was a tiny part of her that was hoping she wouldn't have to. She'd always been better at actions than words. But still... "You're right. We should talk. I want to tell you everything. I just... I got so hung up on—"

"Who were you texting?"

"What?"

"Earlier," said Cami. "The call you got that was so important you just had to take it, who were you talking to?"

Sutton's body tensed, and she narrowed her gaze as the implication slowly set in. "Cam, what are you asking me?"

"You're not answering the question."

"Because I'm not sure it's the one you really want to ask."

"I've been driving myself crazy *for weeks*, Sutton!" Cami's voice pitched up, her stare pained, eyes glossy. "You won't talk to me, and maybe part of it's my own damage. Maybe I'm projecting." She shrugged, shaking her head as her eyes fell shut. "I know. I know you're not Noa. I know we're not my parents, but I am *your wife*. Am I not supposed to question it when you rush off claiming you have doctor's appointments, when you come home smelling like other people—"

"What?"

"—and suddenly start needing to take calls out of earshot?"

"Cami, look at me."

"For all I know you have a terminal illness and the last two weeks has been some kind of misguided romantic attempt to—"

"Camila, *look* at me." Sutton cupped her face, gentle but firm, waiting until their eyes locked. She drew in a breath, grateful when their chests rose and fell in unison, and even then, she didn't try to get the words out—not immediately, not until the tension stretched taut between them began to loosen. "Do you really think I would hide a terminal illness from you?"

"I would never forgive you if you did," said Cami, her voice back to some semblance of normal.

Despite herself, a smile slithered onto Sutton's face, and she shook her head in utter disbelief. There was so much to unpack in everything Cami had said, but she started by reaching into her pocket and offering her phone. "The passcode's still the date you first said you loved me."

Cami's jaw clenched, and she swallowed hard. "I'm not going to look through your phone."

"You should see it for yourself."

"No. I want you to *tell me* what's going on. You can tell me anything. We used to tell each other everything. I don't know why that changed."

"It didn't. I still do. Today was—" Sutton drew in a breath, sliding one hand down Cami's arm to intertwine their fingers and guide her toward the living room. They settled onto the sofa, Sutton folding one leg onto it and taking Cami's hands again, holding her gaze. "The texts, that call I had to take... it was the concierge at that resort in Tahoe. The one we went to that weekend after my first month at Model and you'd just started law school. We hadn't seen each other in three weeks, and I was so desperate to *see* you, to be with you, and not have to think about anything or anyone else."

Cami's expression softened at the memory. "The Landing?"

"Mm-hm." Sutton nodded. "With your vacation starting tomorrow, I thought it might be nice to get away for a day or two. It was supposed to be a surprise. I didn't even think to ask if you'd want to go, which was really fucking selfish now that I think about it."

"*Of course*, I want to go with you."

"But you're right. The timing's off. I promised we'd talk, and instead of telling you what's been going on—" Sutton scoffed at herself, staring down at their joined hands, tracing an arc across the back of Cami's. "I let myself get these ideas, and I fixate. I internalize instead of explaining, and part of me thinks it's because I'm not actually any good at it. Talking. I'm starting to think I'm just scared of what people will say if I do. I'm scared of scaring you."

"You could never..." Cami paused on a heavy exhale, shifting so close their knees were touching. She freed one hand and rested the outside of her index finger beneath Sutton's chin, gently nudging her head up until their eyes met. "Sutton, you could never scare me."

Sutton's gaze pinged skyward, and she swallowed hard, her throat thick with unspoken words. "Something happened when I made director. I can't really explain it. All I know is the first day I was supposed to start, I made it to the parking lot, and I just couldn't get out of the car." She pursed her lips, her shoulders drawing up in a helpless shrug, eyes burning at the mere mention of it. "I couldn't move, not even when my phone started ringing and I saw that it was Luci. Then she called again, and again, and by the time I made myself answer I was already crying and shaking so hard I couldn't even get her name out. So she just stayed on the phone until she drove over to pick me up."

Cami swiped a thumb against her cheek, only then drawing her attention to the tears sitting on the rims of her eyes. "Why didn't you tell me?"

"I wanted to. All I wanted was to pick up the phone and *beg* you to come home so we could fall off the face of the earth together. But I think—I think I also didn't want you to see me like that, and Luci already had. At least once before. The day I graduated USC..." Sutton nipped her top lip, her eyes drifting shut as the memory slipped in. "Remember how she made your entire family come even though they'd already been to her ceremony?"

"Of course. She said your dad and brothers couldn't make it, and Mami and Papi were too happy to sit in their place." Cami rolled her eyes. "They bragged to half the neighborhood how their other daughter was graduating Summa Cum Laude from one of the best business schools in California."

Sutton sniggered, but there was little humor in it. "Michael was the one who couldn't make it. Matthew always does whatever Dad wants, and Dad didn't think it was worth the flight. Not if it was for anything other than med school. He said it would *break*—" Sutton's voice cracked, but she licked her lips, forced a chuckle. "He said it would break my mom's heart, watching me throw away everything to become another admin zombie."

Cami's lips pursed and she nodded, swallowing visibly. "I know I never met your mom, but you always said your dad claimed you were just like her. And I can't believe anyone who's even half the person you are would ever think that."

"I saw her that day," said Sutton.

"How do you mean?" Cami cocked her head, her expression riddled with the confusion of Sutton claiming to have seen someone who died when she was four, nearly two decades later.

"I know it wasn't really *her*, but I saw her face. I don't know if it was a memory or something my brain dredged up from a picture, but I got it in my head that it was some kind of sign. That he was right, that I wasn't where I was supposed to be, that she was angry with me for not following in their footsteps. In hers. Which is absurd, I know—"

"It's not."

"It sounds crazy."

"Baby..." Cami's lips tugged in a sad smile as she shook her head.

"And that look on your face is exactly why—"

Cami leaned in and kissed her, the firm press of their lips grounding Sutton in the moment, slowing her heart rate one beat at a time through the warmth of hands on her face and whispered endearments. After a minute, Cami pulled back with the brush of their noses, their foreheads still touching. "Sorry. I just needed to do that."

"No, I'm sorry." Sutton closed her eyes, holding Cami close, tracing her lips with her thumb. "I'm sorry I didn't tell you. Luce and I never talk about it. Ever. But when she picked me up from work that day, she made me promise to see someone."

"The doctor's appointments," said Cami, her tone steady with understanding. "They're for a therapist."

"Yup. Free of terminal illness," Sutton said through a watery laugh. "Unless you count my proclivity to avoid tough discussions. I mean, I moved two thousand miles across the country so I wouldn't constantly have his voice in my head. So I wouldn't have to listen to how the hospital was my legacy and everyone who knew her tell me how much I look like someone I barely remember, and I *still* saw her that day. I just want to get it all out of my system and not have to talk about any of it for another ten years."

"I don't really think that's how it works," Cami whispered.

"How what works?"

She smoothed a lock of hair behind Sutton's ear, carrying the weight of her reply in the very delay, in the love and concern shimmering in her eyes. "Grief."

Sutton resisted the urge to flinch, to physically reject the implication. "She died when I was four, Cam. I can't remember her laugh, or her favorite food. I barely have a single memory of us together. I don't know what this is, but I wouldn't call it grieving."

"Maybe not, but you still lost her, and I'm sure being raised with whatever ghost of her your dad created didn't make it any better. Either way, I'm glad you finally have someone to help you figure it out."

"I guess. I don't talk about it much. In therapy. I just don't want whatever shook loose in my head to affect *this*." Sutton gestured between them, sitting up straighter. Everything else was preamble—these were the words she needed Cami to hang on to. "I never want to be anything but the best version of myself for you. For *us*. You deserve the world, Cami."

"I love that about you. I love that you give the best of yourself to everyone, even when they don't deserve it. I don't think you know any other way to be, so I'm going to say this as many times as you need to hear it." She stroked the corner of Sutton's mouth with her thumb, staring as if in awe. "I did not say yes to marrying you, wade through months of infuriatingly heteronormative wedding concepts from my parents for a year, promise you for better or worse in front of everyone who matter to us because I only want *the best* of you. I want *you*, Sutton. I. Just. Want. You."

Sutton's shoulders slumped, and she sighed, relief coursing through her. "You always know exactly what to say."

"I don't." Cami's brows drew closer, and she stared down at the space between them. "If I did, I probably would have found a way to tell you how I was feeling before letting the worst thoughts run riot in my head."

"That wasn't on you," said Sutton. "We both know it wasn't."

"Yes, it was, because for a second, for this truly paralyzing moment, I let myself wonder if it was happening again, if I could be so blind..."

Cami's earlier words reverberated in Sutton's mind, and it occurred to her there was still one thing she'd yet to address. When Cami trailed off, pressing both hands to her face and dragging them downward, Sutton caught her by the wrists and gently pulled her hands away. A mislaid buzz thrummed through her, curling her lips in a smile that left Cami frowning, especially when she stood and said, "Hold that thought."

She started in backward steps, one finger held up in promise before she turned and jogged toward their bedroom and into the closet. It took the help of the tiny step stool they kept out of sight, plus standing on the tips of her toes, but she reached for the box on the top shelf of their shoe unit and retrieved the gift bag inside.

Cami's eyes found hers the second she reentered the living room, though Sutton's hands, tucked behind her back, quickly drew her attention. "What are you hiding? I thought we weren't doing gifts until midnight."

"I think I'll have to break the rules just this once, because apparently I've gotten really bad at surprises, or maybe I've always been bad at them." Sutton plopped down onto the couch with a nervous chuckle, resolute, despite the flutter in her stomach. "So bad I've led you to believe I'm either dying or harboring a secret lover."

"Baby—"

"It's okay. I mean, it's not. I hate her for what she did to you. I hate it that she lied, that she cheated. I hate it even more that anything I've done made you question that I could want anyone *but* you," said Sutton, her voice shaky with sincerity. "I don't believe in fate, or destiny, or any of that. At least, I didn't used to, but I don't think it's a coincidence you were sitting in the same bar I happened to stumble into the first night I moved back here. Cam, I left somewhere I'd lived for most of my life, but seeing you that night, talking to you well into the morning, fuck, when you kissed me..." Sutton's eyes fell shut, and it was almost as if she was back there—standing outside the loft teeming with boxes she'd yet to unpack, Cami's hands on her face, lips warm enough to ward off the imminence of fall. "It was the closest I'd ever felt to coming home."

"Sutton..."

She mumbled a swear, shaking her head. "I'm getting completely off track. I just—" She drew both hands onto her lap, Cami's eyes following the small gift bag adorned with purple snowflakes. "I wasn't sure I wanted to give you this."

"Well, now you damn well better." Cami laughed, tears rolling down her face.

Sutton chuckled too, but she reached into the bag to retrieve the oval-shaped crystal bottle, adorned with the words Lavender Haze. "I don't know if this is what you meant about me smelling like someone else. I only wore it once, as a test, but I've also been taking classes for months and trying to shower them off before you get home so you didn't pick up on anything. But it's possible another scent clung to me anyway."

Cami stared at the perfume decanter, in a daze as she cautiously accepted it. "You made this?"

"Yes?" Sutton cringed. "Well, not the bottle. I paid for the packaging, but the fragrance, well, yeah. You've always liked sweeter perfumes, and since you jump from brand to brand instead of just picking one like a normal person, I don't know. I gave it a shot."

"Sutton—"

"I'm not expecting you to love it. I hope you do," she corrected quickly, "but I also wasn't ambitious enough to hinge your entire Christmas present on my amateur perfumery skills, which is why it wasn't under the tree with the rest of them."

Cami's lips found hers, but unlike their last, this kiss didn't come with the desperation of grounding Sutton, conveying security, conviction. It didn't come with the passion-filled rush of the last few nights either, the promise of blunt nails leaving trails down her back, bruises on her neck and thighs. Instead, the soft give and take of their lips, tickle of fingertips along her nape, relief in every breath carried the weight of emotions too big for words. The simplicity and grandeur of *I love you*.

Sutton was the first to come up for air, to breathe Cami in and exhale a laugh. "That's twice tonight. I thought cutting off your rants with kisses was my MO."

"It's criminal that you don't know how fucking perfect you are." Cami's brows twitched, shadows of regret dancing across her face even as her mouth curved in a smile. "But I think I'm the one who's going to need a temporary insanity defense for forgetting."

"I should have told you," said Sutton. "I should've told you all of it."

"I should've trusted you," Cami insisted.

They could probably go back and forth all night, but it all came down to two things, didn't it?

"Trust and communication." Sutton scoffed a laugh. "Sounds familiar." At Cami's confused look, she added, "Something Dr. Copeland said. She likes to slip wholesome marriage tidbits between her maddening notetaking and dissecting all my sentences."

"Please tell me you haven't been giving that woman a hard time for doing her job."

"Never." Sutton slipped the perfume bottle from Cami's hand and onto the coffee table, then reached for Cami, guiding her closer until she was straddling Sutton's hips. "But can we call timeout on the talking? I just want to keep kissing you for a bit."

"A timeout seems in order." Their noses brushed, lips following, but Cami held Sutton's face in both hands, pulling back until their eyes met. "I'm proud of you."

Even in her tender cadence, the declaration hit with a jolt, Sutton's body tensing as if to reject the very validity of it. But her muscles loosened, and her breathing slowed. She still didn't have a ready answer, not for words she'd worked perhaps too hard to earn from someone who'd probably never say them, but this...

Being in the arms of the woman who'd loved her through it all, even when she faltered, got it wrong, failed, she had everything she'd ever needed.

The love of a lifetime, and the most intoxicating *aide-mémoire*.

Home is where the heart is.

Sutton had given her heart to Cami a long time ago. It was still the best decision she'd ever made.

Chapter 12

MERRY CHIPS-MAS

The blend of silk and floral lace beneath Cami's fingertips had always been a heady combination. Last night, after hours of kissing between long overdue talks that ambled into midmorning, she and Sutton had both been too emotionally drained to do anything but stumble through their nighttime routine before drifting off to sleep. But Cami had stirred awake five minutes ago with a subtle tug beneath her navel and the vaguest sentiment that she'd been having the kind of dream she wished she could remember.

Even with the cooler temperature that had settled over the city, the air conditioning in the apartment set at a cozy sixty-five degrees, her skin felt too hot beneath the duvet. It certainly didn't help that she—an unabashed little spoon—had woken with her hips flush to Sutton's ass, one arm low on her hip. The sweet almond scent of body wash flooded her senses, and she gave in to the urge to nuzzle Sutton's neck, press a soft kiss to her shoulder.

Sutton stirred with a sleepy hum, one hand drifting to

Cami's thigh to pull her closer, sending a jolt of awareness to the very tips of Cami's fingers. "You awake?"

"I get the feeling I'm about to be," said Sutton.

Cami feathered a path up her outer thigh, between the small slit of her sleep shorts, reveling in the warmth of her skin beneath the silky fabric. "Have I mentioned how much I love it when you wear these?"

Sutton rolled onto her side, barefaced and beautiful, her hair shielded by a silk wrap, eyes the shade of cinnamon locked on Cami. This early, the rays peeking between their blackout drapes still faint with suggestions of a foggy dawn, not quite alive with the fiery sparks of the sun yet, her laugh was a husky, toe-curling version of itself. "Once or twice."

The new angle gave Cami free rein to run the bridge of her nose along Sutton's jawline, slip her hand beneath the camisole riding up to expose her midriff, and swipe a thumb over her nipple.

"I thought we agreed—*Fuck*, Cami." Sutton tilted her head, arching into Cami's touch. "At least let me go brush my teeth."

Bracing one arm on the bed, Cami hovered over her, smiling as she brushed their lips together. "Five years of waking up next to each other, and you're still worried about morning breath?"

"Only when you clearly have intentions of keeping me here for a while. I'd rather not taste like last night's drool when you kiss me."

"I do love kissing you." Cami punctuated the sentiment by taking Sutton's bottom lip between hers, raking her teeth over it before pulling away. "But I kind of planned on putting my mouth to better use."

Sutton's grip tightened on Cami's waist, squeezing as her

jaw worked, wrestling with undecided words. Her throat bobbed in a hard swallow. She licked her lips. "Did you?"

"Mh-mm." Cami bent her head to kiss a trail down Sutton's neck, along her collarbone to the steel blue decolletage accentuated by the floral trim creating a delicate V across her chest. She pushed at the spaghetti straps and the camisole slipped farther, exposing Sutton's breasts. Cami's mouth watered, but her gaze flicked up at the faint touch of fingers tracing the fine strands along her hairline. She was so hyperaware of Sutton in moments like this—moments when Sutton just looked at her and her heart was on the verge of lurching out of her chest at how surreal it all was. Maybe that was why she'd always been terrified of losing Sutton. Because they were so irreversibly entwined that there were pieces of herself Cami would never get back, that she never wanted back.

"You're so fucking beautiful," Sutton whispered.

And call her basic, but Cami would never get over the way those words sounded leaving Sutton's mouth, the way it made her pulse stutter then sprint. She dipped her chin, swiping her tongue over a hardened nipple before sucking it into her mouth.

"*Ohh.*" Sutton's hand found the back of her head.

Cami's drifted lower, tracing the undefined muscles of Sutton's tensing stomach and slipping into her shorts. She was in no hurry to shift her underwear aside. Instead, she started slow circles, the pressure just enough for Sutton to mewl, part her legs wider.

"Your teeth." Her chest heaved beneath Cami's mouth, the breathy plea in her tone and sheer pleasure unraveling on her face all the clarification Cami needed.

Sutton had always enjoyed breast play—having them touched, kissed, pinched until she was wet and writhing, coming without so much as a touch below the waist. The tangle of labored breaths and moans filling their otherwise silent room told Cami this wouldn't be one of them—they were both too on edge already—but Cami did as she was told and took a nipple between her teeth, just grazing.

"Harder." Her grip tightened in Cami's hair, and it was almost pure instinct, the way Cami responded, moaning as she bit down hard. She compensated by slipping her fingers lower and dragging the waiting arousal up to Sutton's clit. "Fuck, yes."

"Is that good?"

"So good."

Cami's stomach clenched, the throbbing between her thighs driving her to finally slide her hand beneath the band of Sutton's underwear and groan at the glide of her fingers between Sutton's folds. "You're so wet. You're so wet, and I've barely even touched you."

"*Baby*." Sutton tremored, her thighs closing in on Cami's hand as she upped the pressure, making tighter circles on her clit before slipping lower.

And this... This was the moment that always hit the same as that very first night. The one where Cami needed to look Sutton in the eyes, needed to witness the slope of her brows and the way her lips parted when Cami slid inside her. That split second of indecision between fucking her into oblivion or taking her apart unbearably slow. The whimper Sutton let out at the curl of Cami's fingers, the pleading thrust of her hips made up Cami's mind for her.

She worked her fingers deeper, her pace verging on torturous as she kissed a trail toward Sutton's navel. Admittedly, she loved that Sutton exuded dominance with as little as a glance, loved it when she kept her on edge too long, pushed her limits when Cami was sure she couldn't possibly come *one more time*. But there was something in having Sutton so soft, so completely at Cami's will that left her drunk on it every single time.

She pushed at the band of Sutton's shorts, slipping her fingers out to get rid of them completely, despite Sutton's protest.

"No, no, no—Fuck, I was right there."

"You can come." Cami's lips found her inner thigh, and she resisted the urge to smirk when Sutton's other leg drew up, bending at the knee, widening in anticipation. "Just not until I get my tongue on you."

Glossy eyes stared down at her, Sutton's ardent nod like a jolt to Cami's core. "Please."

Her fingers found Sutton's sex again, and her eyes fluttered closed, hips canting, seeking as Cami's breath gusted over her. Everything in Cami yearned to draw it out, to ride this burgeoning pleasure cloud for as long as they could both stand it, but she knew Sutton's body almost as well as she knew her own. Recognized the intensifying quiver of her thighs as Cami lapped at her, the way her hand fumbled along the sheets in search of Cami's, her grasp almost painfully tight when their fingers locked.

Cami moaned at the tightening grip in her hair, dizzy on the taste and smell of Sutton's mounting release, and it was all she could do to press her own hips into the mattress in search of some kind of relief. Heat bore down on her skin, and the vague awareness slipped in that she was still completely dressed, though she'd rid Sutton of most of her clothes. Sutton's hips undulated, and her breath caught.

"Right there. *Right. There.* Fuck, baby, I can't—Cami." Her body went taut, a series of swears and bitten-off moans filling the air as Cami curled her fingers one last time, Sutton clenching around them so tightly Cami had to entirely cease her thrusting. For a second, she just kept them there, long enough for Sutton's muscles to loosen, for her breathing to slow to something verging on normal.

Cami rested her head on Sutton's thigh, catching her breath and waiting for her favorite pair of brown eyes to reemerge. "Merry Christmas."

Sutton dropped her head back in a laugh. "Petitioning to be woken up like this every Christmas. Like, forever."

"I think I could probably make that happen." Their eyes locked again, the tension fraying just enough for the weight of the words to set in. Every breath came laced with sex, sweet almond, and *Sutton*. Cami's pulse refused to slow. It never could whenever Sutton looked at her like this—like nothing existed beyond their ephemeral little bubble of love, laughter, and pure euphoria. She could definitely spend every Christmas like this. *Always*.

Sutton licked her lips, whispered, "Come here," and Cami crawled up to lay next to her. But Sutton had other ideas, curling one arm around Cami's waist and pulling her on top of her. Their lips touched, Cami sighing into the kiss, grinding down when Sutton's leg slipped between her thighs. "You were so good. You were so fucking good, baby."

A knot twisted low in Cami's belly. Whenever Sutton started with praise, she knew she was in trouble. As it was, she was so wet, aching, she was going to come the second Sutton touched her. She had zero delusions about that. It was *after*—when she was still shaking and desperate for more, incoherent pleas tumbling from her mouth—that already had her mind racing with what it would be like. Visions of Sutton disappearing into their closet and reemerging harnessed with Cami's favorite pink dildo was starting to look like a very Merry Christmas indeed.

The doorbell dinged, and Sutton drew back with a frown.

Cami shook her head with shameless urgency, pressing closer and sweeping her tongue into Sutton's mouth. "Ignore it." Everything from the whimper in her tone to her insistent grinding was a dead giveaway.

Bracing one hand on the bed, the other planted low on Cami's back, Sutton sat upright, Cami's arms wrapped around her neck, thighs tightening around her waist. "What do you need?" Sutton tugged at the waistband of Cami's shorts, slipping inside and gliding through her slit, down to her entrance then back. "Tell me what you want and it's yours."

"Inside." Cami gasped, pushing up onto her knees. "I want you inside me. I need—"

Another ding echoed on the wings of Cami's consciousness, poking through the haze of her impending orgasm.

"Are we expecting someone?" Sutton whispered, the rasp in her tone always a bit too much in moments like this, fingers tracing delicate, slippery patterns over Cami's clit, then lower, eyes fixed on Cami as if to decipher every telltale sign of pleasure on her face. The picture of control all while Cami fell to pieces.

"I don't—*fuck*, Sutton." Cami tossed her head back, rolling her hips.

Beneath it all—Sutton's murmured *I love it when you're all worked up like this*, Cami's unhindered moans, the slight ruffle of the duvet against the sheets, an unidentified bird just outside their window—a buzzing stirred. And call it wishful thinking, but the sleek bullet vibrator they kept in the bottom drawer of their nightstand flashed in Cami's mind.

A breathless "Luci," fell from Sutton's lips.

Cami gripped her tighter, nails biting into her shoulders, her back. "Can we not talk about my sister while you're inside me?"

"No, baby. Look." Sutton's hand stilled, and Cami's eyes darted open, the string of protests on her tongue cut off at the sight of Luci's name reflecting on her phone. "It's probably her at the door, and we both know she's not going anywhere until one of us answers."

Cami groaned, every inch of her feverish with need, throbbing from the tips of her fingers to her toes. And really, what would happen if they just decided to not answer, if she stayed right here on Sutton's lap, riding her fingers through messy kisses until she soaked their sheets, until Sutton's name was all she knew? *Sutton, Sutton, Sutton...*

"She has keys, baby." The words hit like a bucket of cold water.

"Fuck." Cami leaned her forehead against Sutton's, resolve seeping in, though the ache hadn't faded one bit. "Why did we ever think that was a good idea?"

"Right now, I can't remember, but..." Sutton licked her lips, tightening the knot in Cami's belly that much more. "We'll see what she wants, then she'll go, and we'll come straight back to bed. And I promise, *I promise* I'll make it so good you won't be able to feel your legs for an hour."

"You know I'm going to hold you to that, right?"

"Good." A smile slid onto Sutton's face, and Cami clenched, whimpering as she slipped her fingers out, kissing a trail to Cami's ear. "Because I can already hear you scream."

With Sutton wearing nothing but the silk camisole dangling off her shoulders and practically all of Cami's clothes still on, it fell to her to answer the door. That didn't mean she was going to be graceful about it. She stomped into the entryway, twisting the locks with unnecessary force before swinging the door open. "Luce, I swear to God this better be—"

"Merry Christmas, Tía!" two small voices chirped in unison.

Cami's eyes darted to the pair of hazel orbs staring up at her, Sofia and Regina garbed in near identical Christmas sweaters, a beaming Minnie Mouse front and center. And okay, maybe she could postpone her annoyance at her sister's questionable timing, considering she'd brought actual angels to her doorstep.

"Hola, mis amores." She knelt, smiling as she pulled the girls into a hug, when a yelp cut her off and a tiny ball of fur shrunk back and scurried behind Luci's legs. She tilted her head for a better look—all golden fur and drooping ears, some kind of golden retriever mix, if she had to guess. "And who's this cutie? I didn't know you were getting a dog."

In fact, if it wasn't for the big dark eyes staring up at her, she'd been sure a puppy was the last thing on Luci and Chema's minds—with two demanding jobs and three kids all under the age of six.

"We didn't get a dog," said Luci.

The honk of a horn drew their attention to the SUV parked by the curb as Chema ducked his head and waved, simultaneously lowering the back window to offer a glimpse of Pablo in his car seat. Cami cooed and wiggled her fingers at her nephew, though he didn't seem to care—too content to babble into the void, tiny hands tapping his feet as he kicked them into the air.

Luci picked up the puppy, waving Chema off with an eye roll Cami recognized all too well seconds before the car took off down the street. Okay. So clearly her sister planned on staying a while, which didn't have to be a problem. She loved Luci, loved her nieces, she reminded herself. Anything to keep her mind from wandering back to five minutes earlier with Sutton's mouth on her neck, and her fingers—

"Where's Tía Sutton?"

Cami blinked at her nieces. Right. The tiny humans on her doorstep. Perfect anaphrodisiac. "Oh, she'll be right out, Regi."

"Out where?"

"Um." A flush bloomed on Cami's cheeks. It never was just one question with kids, was it? "She's... brushing her teeth," she added quickly.

Luci sneered, eyes flicking skyward, and maybe it was big sister's intuition or something, but she'd always been able to see right through Cami. "Please tell me you at least washed your hands."

"Of course, I washed my—" Cami narrowed her gaze, glared at her. "I don't have to explain myself to you. You're the one who showed up unannounced, and you still haven't told me what you're even doing here."

"Chips needs a home," said Sofi, casual.

Cami locked eyes with her older niece. Clearly, she'd misheard. "What's that, honey?"

"Chips, he needs a home."

Right, so her hearing was perfectly fine. She canted her head, eyes trained on her sister again. "Care to explain, Luce?"

"Okay, listen." Luci sighed, her brows sloping apologetically. "We took them to the park because they wanted to see the ducks, and it's the first day off we've both had in forever where we didn't have anywhere else to be. I thought it would be nice."

"Uh-uh." Cami nodded slowly.

"I left Chema alone with them for *two seconds*"—she held up her middle and index fingers for emphasis—"while I fed Pablo, and the next thing I know they're back with *him*." She pointed to the dog.

"So you named him and took him home?" Cami balked. Moments like this, it was difficult to remember *she* was supposed to be the impulsive one. Dramatic, emotional, all heart before reason. Showing up at someone's house at barely nine a.m. on Christmas morning with stray puppies in tow was not becoming of her pragmatic, get-shit-done older sister. "How do we know he doesn't belong to anyone?"

"No collar, underfed, dirty fur—"

"Right, right." Cami held up a hand to cut her off. "None of that explains why you brought him *here*."

"We told the girls we'd take him to a shelter, but—"

"But you'll keep him, right, Tía? You and Tía Sutton," Sofi chimed in.

The burst of optimism in her voice, never mind the tiny, imploring hand tugging at the hem of Cami's shirt, Regi beaming up at her expectantly, silently waiting... It was all too much. And as far as dirty tricks went, this had to be the lowest. Cami huffed out a heavy breath, locking eyes with Luci again. "You know Sutton doesn't do pets."

"Tía Sutton doesn't like dogs?" Sofi's voice echoed outrage.

Cami cradled her face with a placating hand. "No, honey, she loves dogs."

"Is she allergic?"

"To mess," Cami grumbled.

Sofi and Regi just looked confused.

"Sof, why don't you and Regi take Chips to the living room for a while? I need to talk to your mom."

Luci handed off the dog to her older daughter, but he immediately wiggled out of her grip, tiny paws scuffling across hardwood as they chased after him.

"Am I seeing things, or is there a puppy here?" Sutton emerged next to them, fresh faced and completely dressed, perplexity creasing the skin between her brows.

"Regina!" Sofi screamed.

The puppy yipped, scurrying away as Regi released his ear.

"Yeah, you two are obviously in the middle of something, but clearly someone needs to keep an eye on that." Sutton hooked a thumb over her shoulder, already backing away.

Cami and Luci loitered at the edge of the entryway, a smile dancing on the wings of Cami's lips as she watched Sutton get on all fours and duck her head to coax Chips out from under the coffee table.

"I'm guessing things are better," said Luci, drawing Cami's focus. "I mean, I figured they already were yesterday when Sutton showed up with the"—she gestured haphazardly to her own neck—"bee sting, was it?"

Cami shot her a look, but they both laughed.

"Then you were weird all through the cookie contest and dinner, and you two left before I could ask either of you about it, but that look on your face..." Luci trailed off. "The dopey, nauseating thing you're doing right now. That's what gave it away the first time."

Cami blinked, frowned. "Gave what away?"

"That you were in love with her. Back then, I mean."

Oh. Cami sighed, shaking her head to clear the fog in

her brain. Given how they'd left things at Dolce last week, how she'd practically pleaded for Luci to tell her whether Sutton was hiding some torrid love affair, the least she could do was update her about the talk she and Sutton had had last night. "Look, Luce, the other day at Dolce, there was a lot I didn't know. Between everything with Mami and Papi, especially with Sutton and I, I guess it just felt like the floor has been slipping out from under me for weeks."

Luci nodded, mulling over the words, gaze drifting to the space between them, then back to Cami's. "I know we grew up thinking we knew exactly what love is supposed to look like, thinking we knew exactly what we wanted, but I'm starting to realize there's no blueprint to marriage, Cam. Falling in love, falling hard and fast... That's the easy part. It's everything between that makes a marriage. Knowing someone at their best and worst, navigating everything that makes life as fucking tedious as it is beautiful, and still choosing, wanting, that person at the end of it all. That's marriage. And you and Sutton, you're not Mami and Papi, okay? You get to write your own story."

"I know." Cami bobbed her head in agreement, already moving in for a hug. "And thank you."

Luci scoffed, never able to resist a bit of blasé whenever things got too soppy. "For ruining Christmas in bed with your wife?"

"For loving her the way you love me," said Cami. "For being there. Getting her to see Dr. Copeland."

Luci shook her head, but her arms tightened around Cami. "She did it for you. For herself too, but—"

"I know. I'm still glad she has you. That we both do." Cami pulled away, hands gripping Luci's shoulders as she looked her dead in the eyes. "But you know neither of us are talking her into keeping that dog, right?"

"I'm... not so sure." Luci grinned, pointing toward the living room. "You underestimate how good Sofi and Regi are at getting their way. Plus, we all know Sutton is terrible at telling them no."

Cami burbled a laugh. She'd never bet on her being the tough parent somewhere down the line, but every time she saw Sutton with the girls or Pablo, she envisioned a future of Sutton whisking her out of the kids' earshot to make entreaties on their behalf. Five more minutes of TV, telescopes for Christmas, and expensive cameras for their birthday. Nights when she'd build pillow forts in their bedroom, just to make them smile.

Her eyes flicked up, darting between Cami and Luci before she whispered something to Sofi and Regi and left Chips in their care. "Could you..."

"Go," said Luci, already moving to pick up where Sutton had left off. "I'll make sure he doesn't chew on your fancy couch cushions."

"You better. Also"—Sutton aimed a finger at her—"don't think you're off the hook for this because your kids are cute."

"Wouldn't dream of it," Luci sang, not the least bit threatened.

Without another word, Sutton rested her hand on the small of Cami's back, guiding her toward their bedroom and slipping inside, leaving the door slightly ajar. She turned, eyes wide and brows raised as they came face to face. "A dog?"

"I know. It's crazy," said Cami.

"They're *a lot* of responsibility."

"They are..."

"He probably hasn't had a checkup or shots, so we'd obviously need a good vet." Sutton pressed a hand to her temple, pacing for a few steps before dropping her hand as shock screeched onto her face all over again. "A bed and toys and feeding bowls. Places for his bed and toys and feeding bowls."

Cami smiled, too amused, too endeared, to even attempt to intervene.

"He doesn't even have a name! A proper name anyway." Sutton halted her strides, turned to Cami. "Are we really calling him Chips?"

Cami bit her bottom lip, slinking closer to wrap both arms around Sutton's neck. "You want to keep him."

"*Want* is a strong word." Sutton's nose twitched with a grimace. "It's just—We can't give him away after Luci practically dropped him on our doorstep with his big, sad eyes and stupid adorable face."

"Baby—"

"Plus, finding the right shelter is complicated. Do you know there are animals that never get to leave? They just live their whole lives in a tiny cage until—" She stuck her head out the door, almost as if to check neither the kids nor the puppy could hear her. "Until eventually they just get put down," she finished in a whisper.

"We don't know that that will happen." Cami laughed. "I'm sure there are lots of shelters in the city with high enough placement rates, or that will take great care of him."

"We have to keep him," Sutton blurted.

"We do?" Cami hedged, only now allowing the hope burgeoning in her chest to take flight.

"Yeah. Right?" Sutton questioned, a calm seeming to settle over her. "My gym instructor Whitney has a dog, and I bet she knows a good vet. Maybe even groomers, and a great pet store. Fuck." Her eyes fell shut, and she breathed a laugh. “I had plans for us this week. Now my brain’s stuck on doggy daycare math.”

“Firstly…” Cami dipped her chin, brushing her mouth against Sutton’s. “Very, very intrigued by these plans. Second.” She shook her head, smile never leaving her face, feeling so content, so weightless she could just float away without the hands on her hips to ground her. “We’ll figure it out. Whatever he needs, we’ve got this, right?”

Sutton hummed, pulling Cami closer as her lips curled in a grin. “Damn right we do.”

Chapter 13

DRIFTWOOD

SUTTON DAVIES (8:37 P.M.)

Are you there?

Does she suspect anything?

JUSTIN NICHOLS (8:38 P.M.)

We're by the bar just like you told me, but she's restless.

Pretty sure she's already dying to go home to you and Chips.

Lesbians 🙄

SUTTON DAVIES (8:39 P.M.)

Bi-erasure 🚨

Besides, you and Brady are the ones who practically U-Hauled so jokes on you.

JUSTIN NICHOLS (8:39 P.M.)

We did not U-Haul!

SUTTON DAVIES (8:40 P.M.)

Sure.

My rideshare is pulling up.

Get off your phone before she sees you texting me.

JUSTIN NICHOLS (8:41 P.M.)

No good deed 😩

SUTTON DAVIES (8:41 P.M.)

Love you too, Nichols 😘

Sutton clicked her screen dark and slipped her phone into the pocket of her coat—the same one she'd been wearing all those years ago, the wool only further softened with time, its ivory shade no less pristine thanks to hundreds of dollars spent on dry cleaning bills. Beyond the window, the blur of buildings began to settle as the car slowed, her eyes zoning in on worn red bricks only lit by a pair of vintage wall sconces.

"Have a good night," her driver droned.

She mumbled a halfhearted *thanks, you too* and exited onto the curb. The street hummed with chatter and the moderate flow of traffic behind her, sirens always somewhere in the distance. A neon yellow and green sign advertising Mexican food glowed in the window of the next building, though the blend of herbs and spices hovering beneath the pervading car exhaust was always a pleasant giveaway.

It had been years since she'd stumbled into Driftwood that night, but somehow nothing had changed. She was grateful to find that the interior was just the same. All brick walls, wooden two tops and stools down the middle, a long U-shaped bar crowded with patrons, and equally crammed booth seats along the back. The scent of cheesy fries and potato skins danced with the ever-present odors of beer and sweat. No one could ever accuse this dingy little dive of being classy, but Sutton would always carry pieces of it in her heart.

Five years ago, she'd been too distracted, checking her phone to see whether she was in the right place to identify the exact moment Cami had noticed her. Tonight, she couldn't tear her gaze away, catching the very moment Justin squeezed Cami's arm, whispering something beneath the blare of soft rock as he pointed Sutton's way.

Cami canted her head, squinting as she stood and started toward Sutton. The stylish mock neck sweater she wore with frost white jeans and boots was a far cry from the cozy half-zip she'd donned that night, but everything from her tentative steps to the adorable frown on her face was so achingly familiar. "Babe?"

"Cami." Sutton smiled, slipping into character with a surprised shake of her head. "I thought that was you."

Cami grimaced, flinching. "What? What are you doing here? Is everything okay?"

Sutton's eyes swept the bar from one corner to the next as if she wasn't quite sure how she managed to stumble inside either. After all, last time she'd been there, before she'd accepted a job at Model and undertaken a permanent move to San Francisco, espresso machines lined the barback, imbuing the air with coffee and caramel. The crowd had been a perpetual assortment of artsy and hipster types conferring over laptops across ash wood tables, obscure indie songs forever streaming in the background. "Didn't this used to be a coffee shop?"

"Wha—*ohh*." Cami dropped her head back, lips quirking in a smile as realization finally came over her. A surprise date dedicated to the night they'd begun might've seemed bizarre, pointless to anyone else, but Cami didn't miss a beat. "Is this the part where I say, 'it did. A year ago. But I meant *here*, San Francisco.'"

"Right." Sutton breathed a laugh, the words flooding her memories as if she'd only lived this moment yesterday. "I moved. Or… moved back?"

"You did? Luci didn't mention anything."

"That's because she doesn't know yet." Sutton glanced down at her booties, tapping one heel against the already scuffed wooden floor before she met Cami's waiting stare. "I'm going to tell her, but I only got back today, and it's my birthday, which should probably—"

"It's your birthday?" Cami looked away for a second, brows drawn low as she blinked in consideration, just like she had that night. Sutton bit down on a smile—her wife never could half-ass anything. "September 12th," said Cami, so softly Sutton wasn't sure she was meant to hear it. "Fuck, it is your birthday. And you're spending it alone?"

"I don't mind being alone." Sometimes she even preferred it.

"Let me buy you a drink." Cami scrunched up her face. "Is that—I mean, *do you* drink?"

"Only more wine than I probably should. But I should actually head home. I still have a lot of unpacking to do."

"Unpacking? On your birthday? I can't let you do that."

"Camila." Sutton couldn't explain it, not until much later that night, but there was something in the way Cami visibly drew in a breath then, lips slightly parted, stare unflinching, that sent Sutton back to summers spent with Luci at their parents' house. All those days they'd run into each other in the basement, Sutton often carrying a load of laundry, Cami grabbing something from the deep freeze, her eyes always lingering a bit too long.

Cami stepped closer, fingers trailing the lapels of

Sutton's coat. "Do you know what hearing you say my name like that did to me even then?"

A bemused smile glided onto Sutton's face. "That's not what you're supposed to say."

"No. This is the part where you're all aloof and sexy, definitely a little sad, and you expect me to just watch you walk out of here."

"Well, that lasted a solid thirty seconds." She hadn't expected Cami to rush out after her, halfway down the street when a call of her name turned her around, holding her in place until Cami caught up with a jog that left her breathless, unsure what she even wanted to say. Not that Sutton knew either.

"God, I thought I would explode with how flustered and awkward I was, and you were so—" Cami gritted her teeth, groaning in mock frustration before whispering against Sutton's mouth. "But I couldn't... I couldn't just let you leave."

"Every day I'm glad you didn't." She draped her arms around Cami's neck, capturing her lips in a tender kiss, reveling in the closeness of her, the significance of standing in the bar that changed their lives, and knowing there wasn't a single thing she'd do differently.

"Kissing already?" Cami pulled back enough for their eyes to meet, her grip still tight on Sutton's jacket. "We're way off script."

"I think I made my point." Sutton beamed. To anyone who'd noticed them standing in the middle of the bar, she probably looked as lovestruck as she felt. She just couldn't bring herself to care. "Do you want to grab a table and get some food? Or we could stick to the source material, go for that walk."

Cami slipped her hand into Sutton's, intertwining their fingers as if it was the easiest choice she'd ever had to make. "Let's walk. I feel like we haven't taken a walk together in forever."

"Sounds perfect." Sutton sealed the decision with one last press of her lips to Cami's before lifting her gaze toward the bar to find Justin watching them with a smile. She bobbed her head, indicating that they were heading out—a possibility they'd already discussed when he agreed to get Cami to the bar for her—and he tipped his drink toward them in acknowledgment. For all his veiled commentary about Cami dying to go home to Sutton and Chips, he was probably already anxious to be home with Brady too.

They exited the bar and wordlessly headed down Stevenson Street, Cami's arm looped around Sutton's as they walked. It wasn't quite as drastic as growing up in New York, but that night, as they strolled unwittingly toward the pier, she'd found herself taking note of the change in the air, the shift between summer and fall. How she'd miss the yellows, reds, and purples, the serenity of pink-streaked sunsets viewed from Central Park. With Cami next to her, she'd missed it all a little less. Tonight, that was no less true.

"Chips!" Cami blurted, completely shattering the tranquility of the moment. She turned, eyes widened. "Should we be leaving him alone already?"

"He's fine." Sutton couldn't help but laugh. "Luci's got him. She agreed to keep him both nights we're in Tahoe too, considering she did kind of thrust us into pet parenthood the very week I planned on sweeping you off your feet." She rolled her eyes and released a bashful sigh riddled with mirth. "Trying to anyway."

Cami's expression softened, and they came to a

complete halt in the middle of the sidewalk, beneath the expanse of a starless oblivion, the blitz of headlights on zooming cars leaving her tawny complexion aglow every few seconds. "You've never needed to try. Sutton, I love you so much, even at our worst, it's the idea of losing you that's so crushing I forget to breathe. All of this..." She paused, smiling down at their linked hands. "The tree, the baking and dinners, specialty perfumes, first date do overs and Tahoe, it's incredible. I know gestures are your way of putting it all into words sometimes—how you say you're sorry, how you say you love me, and I love that. I just hope you know I don't *need* it."

"I know." Sutton nodded, her chest clenching at the underlying meaning.

Cami's hand found her cheek. "You don't have to prove yourself to me, or anyone."

Her throat tightened, eyes stinging at the unexpected rush of emotion. That didn't mean she didn't still want to—prove herself. Logically, she knew not every day could be like being home for the holidays. Work happened. Life happened. And she wasn't sure what the latter had in store, but she couldn't imagine doing it with anyone *but* Cami.

"There are lots of things I don't know," said Sutton. "Whether my dad will ever change, if things would've been different if my mom was still alive, if I even want the job I worked so hard to land, or if I'm just predisposed to chasing the next rational accomplishment. What I do know is... I never want to lose sight of this again. Not for anything. I'm not promising rainbows and sunshine, but I promise to walk the dog when you're tired. To do that head rub thing you like whenever you can't sleep. And yes, sometimes I'll cook dinner before you're home and plan secret rendezvous to anywhere from dive bars fifteen minutes away to the next fucking continent, because I love you, Cami." She closed her eyes, squeezing Cami's hand tighter as she pressed it over her racing heart. "And I promise to love you until my heart stops beating."

A faint catch of breath echoed between them, the seconds stretching as Cami held her closer, eyes gleaming and lips curled in a smile. "Why do I feel like you just rewrote your vows on a random Tuesday in the middle of Downtown?"

Sutton's stomach flipped at the prospect. "Not exactly what I was going for, but if it keeps that smile on your face we can come back next week and do it all over again."

"You're ridiculous."

"Only for you."

Cami tugged her bottom lip between her teeth, though it did nothing to suppress the grin beaming through. "Keep talking to me like this and we might have to skip the rest of this walk and fast forward to the part where you invite me in."

"On the first night?" Sutton's jaw dropped in mock outrage.

But Cami simply leaned closer, whispered, "I know. A true scandal."

Their noses touched, Sutton's every breath laced with lavender. "I never did stand a chance after you kissed me."

"Is that your way of saying I should kiss you now?"

"I mean..." She shrugged, her pulse racing at the brush of their lips. "It couldn't hurt."

In so many ways, that night had felt more like a culmination of something that had been simmering beneath the surface for years—unspoken, but ever present. Maybe she'd just been afraid to look too closely, to name it. She didn't believe in kismet, didn't believe her future was written in the stars, but she couldn't help feeling like this was where she was always meant to be—this city, snug in these arms, with lips that always tasted like home pressed to hers.

She didn't believe in kismet.

But maybe she was starting to.

Keep Reading

Want more Cami & Sutton? Keep reading for a glimpse of what they're up to one year later.

Lovers of the *Gia, San Francisco series*, this one is especially for you! 💖

Bonus Chapter

NEW YEAR'S EVE

one year later

An electropop hit streamed into the night as Cami deposited her empty champagne flute onto a passing tray and leaned against the glass balustrade. A gentle breeze swept through, the deep neckline and thin, rhinestone-adorned fabric of her jumpsuit only doing so much to stave off the chill, but the patio heaters positioned across Gia's rooftop lent the perfect balance to ring in the New Year outdoors.

Cocktail waiters garbed in black and white weaved through the mingling guests—lawyers from Dimaano, external colleagues, family, and friends all aglow with the buzz of an open bar and aesthetic light fixtures gilding each table. Everything from the glimpse of Golden Gate Bridge and the panoramic skyline splayed out behind her, to the cozy, cream-colored booths skirting the rooftop's perimeter alongside impeccably tended plants attested to the sheer indulgence of the night.

Leave it to Pedro Dimaano to throw a glorified office mixer at one of the most sought-after restaurants on the West Coast, reserving not one, but both private dining spaces for the occasion. Food, drinks, and conversation on the rooftop, charity poker and blackjack in "Private Dining 2."

As she continued to sweep the space, Cami's eyes found Sutton, standing amid a rapidly expanding group, Pedro's younger daughter Whitney—Sutton's gym instructor turned friend—at the center of it. Years of negotiating contracts, never mind heading her own department had equipped Sutton to confer with almost anyone, but her brain had never failed to draw the distinction between work and being social. If the poker chip dancing between her fingers, a conduit for all her nervous energy, was anything to go by, schmoozing at parties still made her the slightest bit anxious.

"Trying to decide whether she needs rescuing?"

Cami spun to find Avery, Pedro's eldest daughter, emerge next to her, the spine of a wine glass gracefully caught between her fingers. A certified lawyer herself, she'd come through the firm fairly often over the years, but had opted for a career in restaurant admin and human resources, to Pedro's dismay. Although, it probably hadn't hurt when he set his sights on the very restaurant she worked in for tonight's party.

Cami chuckled, her eyes flicking back to Sutton. "Is it that obvious?"

"Only because of that thing she's doing with the poker chip. Andy, Whit's girlfriend..." Avery tipped her glass toward a striking Black woman next to Whitney, pixie cut styled in a perfect swoop against her forehead. "She does the same thing whenever she's nervous. Latches on to some unassuming thing to fidget with and prays no one catches on."

Cami gave an amused tilt of her head, narrowing her eyes at Avery. "Yeah, Sutton *has* mentioned that, but I've never actually seen Andy look like anything less than the coolest person in the room."

"Meh. The leather jackets do a lot of heavy lifting. Also" —Avery lightly tapped herself on the forehead—"of course you know Andy. Sorry. Sometimes I forget that half the queer women in a city-wide radius *do* actually know each other."

"Right?" Cami laughed, silently deliberating whether to elaborate before adding, "My sister got us a puppy last year, and Whitney's sort of been our go-to dog mom, which spiraled into these weird double date hang outs with our dogs. Then Sutton and Andy started hanging out, and now I'm pretty sure they have their own recovering perfectionist support group going on."

Avery squeezed Cami's arm, her eyes alight with intrigue and something verging on conspiratorial glee. "Please tell me Jenn is already in on that."

"What am I meant to be in on?" The silky affectation in her tone gave away her presence seconds before Jenn Coleman glided to a halt next to them. Hands hidden within the pockets of tailored beige slacks, her eyes wandered, assessing their surroundings the way only a famously meticulous chef standing in her own restaurant would.

Avery didn't miss a beat. "Andy and Sutton's recovering perfectionist group."

"Oh." Jenn's frown deepened as she turned to regard Avery then Cami. "We meet on Sundays for smoothies at W. Cami knows that."

"Okay, why is it less funny when *you* joke about it?" said Avery.

"Who's joking?" Jenn's lips quirked with the faintest hint of a smile, but she glanced at her watch, then mumbled, "I should get back to the kitchen. It was nice to see you, Cami. Ave, can you check on Private Dining 2?"

"We're not supposed to be working tonight!" Avery called out, but Jenn was already weaving through the crowd toward the stairs.

Cami bit down on a laugh. She'd only met Jenn twice—once in passing while she and Sutton had been having dinner at Gia, and the other when she'd catered Brady and Justin's wedding. Still... "Something tells me she's always this intense."

"Oh, a hundred percent," said Avery. "The only reason she even let my dad throw this spectacle here is because I agreed to take care of everything except menu planning."

"I mean, I have to admit when Pedro said he wanted to take the firm's New Year party offsite this year, I was imagining something a little... stuffier." Cami resisted the urge to grimace. "Like, the overpriced ballroom of some luxury hotel."

"Yeah, well, he wanted Gia and Jenn hates catering, so this was the happy middle ground, with the caveat that proceeds from the casino games go to a charity for LGBTQ+ teens."

Cami swiped a full glass from the tray as a waiter paused in front of them, mumbling a quick thanks before turning to clink her glass against Avery's. "Love that." If she was going to be swayed into losing money at poker of all things, she couldn't think of a better cause.

"Sorry. Let me just..." Avery held up a finger, despite the wine glass still caught in her grip, and Cami frowned before taking note of the buzzing phone in her other hand, the caller ID lit up with the name Ky and a purple heart. Her face scrunched up with regret as she glanced at Cami again. "I need to take this. Her flight got delayed, but she's still trying to make it here, even though she should definitely be home resting after *two* connections —"

Cami waved off the explanation with a smile. "Go. We'll catch up later if you're still around."

"Or if you are." Avery bobbed her head toward something, her phone halfway to her ear as she started walking away.

Cami followed the directive to find Sutton rushing toward them, her clutch tight in one hand, her strapless satin gown pinched between the thumb and index finger of her other, the rippled ruching and slit running up one leg accentuating every curve. Even after watching her get dressed earlier—every step from the lacy black thong she'd slipped on to the pair of heeled sandals on her feet—Cami's pulse still stuttered at the sight of her. She paused, pushing straightened raven locks behind her ear as she trained expectant dark eyes on Cami. "It's time."

"Time?" Cami uttered.

"For the..." Sutton made an indistinct gesture with her hands, prompting Cami to tilt her head in a futile attempt to decipher it.

"Two fingers... a trigger?" Cami sputtered a laugh, swiftly abandoning the quest. "You're being adorably incoherent right now, but I'm really going to need you to use your words."

Sutton huffed, slipping her hand into Cami's and plastering on a smile as she wove through a throng of Cami's colleagues, Justin's booming laugh in the thick of it, and into the stairway. Their heels clacked on hardwood, Cami still chuckling as she did her best to keep up.

"Where are we going?" she asked.

"Somewhere private," Sutton hissed. Like clockwork, a waiter carrying a tray of artfully arranged canapes stepped onto the landing, forcing her to duck her head as he raised his arm to a safe height.

Cami mimicked the maneuver, following as they started down a dimly lit hallway and Sutton pushed at the first door on the right, pulling her inside before shutting the door. Darkness greeted them, the scent of detergent and bleach filling her nose seconds before a fluorescent bulb flicked on, revealing an organized array of brooms, mops, and marked bottles of cleaning supplies.

"This is..." Sutton's brows dipped as she turned, scrutinizing the space. "Not a bathroom."

"Well, no, babe," Cami said through a laugh. "Because the bathrooms are probably still where they were the last time we were here." She reached for Sutton's hips, guiding her closer, all but eliminating the last sliver of space between them as she whispered, "Not that I can't still get on board if this is a seduction mission."

Sutton hummed, her hands fumbling with the clasp of her clutch even as her breath gusted over Cami's lips. "Might be, if poking me with needles is a new kink you forgot to mention."

"*Ohh.*" Cami's jaw slackened, her eyes wide as her gaze fell to the mini medicine cooler in Sutton's hand. "*That* time."

"Yes, that time." Mirth danced in Sutton's eyes, but she shook her head. "You have a one-track mind."

"Because you were so well behaved the last time we were alone in a supply closet."

"You started that," Sutton argued.

"Finished too," said Cami. "Twice, if I remember."

"You're impossible."

Cami laughed, her smile gradually fading as she took the needle, watching as Sutton placed her clutch on a free-standing shelf and ripped open an alcohol pad. Even after two days of these injections, it had slipped Cami's mind, standing on a rooftop with colleagues, music, and the imminence of New Year fireworks all around. From everything their fertility specialist had told them, their chances of conceiving were relatively high with IVF, even considering Sutton had been diagnosed with PCOS in her teens. They'd done the reading, sat through countless info-sessions and meetings with their doctor, enough to know the journey to having their first child may not always be easy. Cami still couldn't think of anyone else she'd rather be stuck in a supply closet with. She was never getting off this ride.

Sutton pulled up her dress and swiped the alcohol pad over a spot just left of her navel, the look in her eyes softening as she glanced up and found Cami watching. "What?"

"Nothing." Cami's grin turned undoubtedly dopey as she uncapped the needle. "I'm just ridiculously in love with you."

"Yeah?" Sutton beamed. "Is this doing it for you? Seeing me all disheveled in a tiny room with bad lighting?"

"It is, a little bit. But you know that's not what I meant."

"I know," said Sutton, softer now. She released her dress to stand upright and close the gap between them. Their mouths brushed. "Because I happen to be ridiculously in love with you too."

"Kissing you with this thing in my hand feels a little haz—"

The door swung open, revealing a woman garbed in a

pristine chef's coat, brunette hair hidden beneath her cap, though a few errant strands dangled on either side of her face. Her eyes darted to the syringe in Cami's hand before sweeping up to their faces. She paused, gears clearly turning in her mind, then held up a hand and shook her head. "I'm sure this is not what it looks like. Actually"—she canted her head—"I'm not sure I've decided what this looks like."

"Val!" someone yelled, their voice carrying from down the hallway.

"On it!" Val blared over her shoulder before facing them again. "Can you—" She waved her hand in a beckoning motion toward a trio of brooms.

Sutton wordlessly reached for the one with the green handle and passed it to her.

"I'm going to close this since you two were clearly in the middle of something." Val took a step back, pulling the door halfway shut only to swing it open again. "Just... Please don't have sex in here. Jenn is very particular about where people get naked in her restaurant. Like, lifetime ban particular."

Cami sputtered a laugh. "I'm sure she is, but don't worry. We promise everyone's clothes will stay on."

Val narrowed her gaze. "That's... only mildly reassuring."

"Val, was it?" Sutton interjected, her face the picture of agreeable despite the laughter in her tone. "We promise not to have sex in here. She just needs to poke me with that needle, and we're done. Two minutes. Scouts honor."

Cami gave an ardent nod, pointing at Sutton with her free hand. "Said by an *actual* girl scout, Val."

"Fine." Val laughed, shaking her head as she started to close the door again. "Have a good night you two."

Their *thanks, you too* rang out in unison, spurring another fit of laughter between them. This would definitely be one of those stories they told on Nochebuena in a year or two, one they'd maybe even tell their kids.

Whenever Cami looked back, as far as she could remember, she still couldn't pinpoint the moment her parents realized they were better friends than lovers. Even after a year of evolving communication and intimacy in her marriage, embarking on her own journey with therapy, she wasn't sure she knew the secret to thirty years. A lifetime. But if she did get so lucky to be asked one day, she'd say the secret was being best friends *and* lovers. An unquenchable lust for getting to know each other, even still. Being willing to get a lot of things wrong before getting them right. It was realizing even a perfect love wasn't without flaws, wasn't always effortless or glamorous, and knowing none of that made it any less real. Any less extraordinary.

She raised her hand to Sutton's cheek, tracing the hinge of her jaw as their foreheads touched. "Where were we?"

Sutton smiled, her sigh so soft, near dreamlike when she said, "Making a baby?"

Cami chuckled—stomach fluttering, heart hammering at the very prospect—and she whispered the words against Sutton's mouth, "Let's make a baby."

Thank You

Thank you for reading ***NOCHEBUENA***!

If you enjoyed Cami & Sutton's journey to rediscovering romance, please consider leaving a review by clicking the links below!

Amazon

Goodreads

For updates on upcoming projects, bonus chapters, sneak peeks, and giveaways, subscribe to my newsletter or follow me on Instagram, Twitter, or Facebook.

Never miss a sale or a new book release!

FOLLOW ME ON BOOKBUB

Please remember to take breaks and be kind to yourselves.

— STEPH 

Also by Stephanie Shea

Whispering Oaks: a wlw romantic suspense

Liquid Courage

Collide: a Flippin' Fantastic romance

Avalanche: a queer romance novelette

Apt 103: a queer romance short story

The Gia, San Francisco Romance Series:

Chef's Kiss

Missed Connection

Take Two

About the Author

Stephanie Shea is a self-proclaimed introvert, who spent her days in corporate daydreaming of becoming a full-time novelist.

Her favorite things include binging TV shows, creating worlds where no character is too queer, broken or sensitive, and snacks. Lots of snacks.

Someday, she hopes to curb her road rage and get past her anxiety over social media and author bios.

stephaniesheawrites.com

Printed in Great Britain
by Amazon